By Ditter Kellen

www.ditterkellen.com

Copyright © Ditter Kellen

All rights reserved. This copy is intended for the original purchaser of this book ONLY. No part of this book may be reproduced, scanned, or distributed in any printed or electronic form without prior written permission from Ditter Kellen. Please do not participate in or encourage piracy of copyrighted materials in violation of the author's rights. Purchase only authorized editions.

Image/art disclaimer: Licensed material is being used for illustrative purposes only. Any person depicted in the licensed material is a model.

Published in the United States of America.

Ditter Kellen

P.O. Box 124

Highland Home, AL, 36041

This book is a work of fiction. While reference might be made to actual historical events or existing locations, the names, characters, places, and incidents are either the product of the author's imagination or are used fictitiously, and any resemblance to actual persons, living or dead, business establishments, events, or locales are entirely coincidental.

Warning

This book contains scenes that may be considered triggers to some readers.

Dedication

To my beautiful friend, Cathe Green, who held my hand and cracked the whip when I needed it. If not for her keeping me grounded, I would have changed the ending to this book a dozen times. Thank you, Cathe, my sister, my heart, for believing in me. I love you BIG.

Acknowledgement

A big thank-you to Andy Bingham for beta reading this story and for loving the twisted as much as I do!

A huge thanks to retired deputy Tommy Cook for his help with police protocol and procedures.

Research links used for suppressed memories and the neurobiology of abused children.

https://news.northwestern.edu/stories/2015/08/traumatic-memories-hide-retrieve-them

http://www.dana.org/Cerebrum/2000/Wounds_That_Time_Won%E2%80%99t_Heal__The_Neurobiology_of_Child_Abuse/

Prologue

Wexler, Alabama

Population 2415

"Elle!" Elijah Griffin shouted, the back door slamming in the distance, a testament to his mood.

He'd been drinking again.

Elenore hovered behind the chicken coop, her bare feet catching on briars in her haste to escape her father.

"Elle Griffin? So help me God, girl, I will take my belt to you if you don't bring your butt here at once!"

She didn't want to leave the safety the shadows of the chicken coop provided. But she was afraid not to.

If she remained there, and her father found her hiding from him, he would hurt her. Badly.

Tears gathered in her eyes, but she blinked them back. One thing Elijah Griffin hated worse than disobedience was tears.

Elenore wiped at her eyes with the hem of her dress and stepped from behind the coop.

The evening sun had begun its descent, casting shadows along the side of the house and hiding her father's expression from view.

But Elenore didn't need to see his face to understand what he wanted from her, what he'd been taking from her for years.

She lowered her head and slowly moved in his direction.

"Where've you been, girl?" He gripped her upper arm in a painful hold. "Get your butt in that house."

Elenore stumbled toward the steps at the back door. She swallowed back the panic that rose in her throat at the knowledge of the horror that awaited her inside.

She could feel her father tight on her heels, knew he would be on her within seconds.

But hard as she tried, Elenore could fight the tears no longer.

And the tears would make it worse…so much worse.

"Are you crying?" he slurred, his hand suddenly in her hair.

He jerked her around to face him. "What have I told you about crybabies?"

"I-I won't do it again."

He stared at her for achingly long moments, unsteady on his feet. "Get in your room."

Elenore didn't want to go into her room. She knew what would happen to her once inside.

He backhanded her across the face.

The copper taste of blood filled her mouth.

With her jaw now throbbing to the beat of her heart, Elenore staggered toward her bedroom door, Elijah following close behind.

She could hear the buckle of his belt tinkering as he released it and slid it free of his beltloops. She turned to face him.

"Take it off," he demanded, nodding to her dress.

Her fingers trembled so badly they barely functioned.

He took a step toward her. "Now!"

Elenore jumped, lifting her shaky fingers to the first button at the top of her dress.

There would be no stopping her father from what he intended to do to her. There never was.

Elenore took a slow, deep breath, lifting her gaze to a place just beyond his shoulder. She forced her eyes to relax until the wall behind him faded into the distance. Her vision grew tunneled, and her mind floated off to a place where nothing or no one could touch her. Especially not her father…

Chapter One

Ten Years Later

Elenore kept her gaze on the floor and accepted the two bags of groceries the bag boy handed her.

"Do you need some help carrying them to your car?"

She knew the bag boy spoke to her, but she pretended not to hear him. Besides, if he saw that she didn't have a car, there would be no hiding the pity that would surely come.

And Elenore hated pity, nearly as much as she despised her father's pet name for her. *Elle.* It wasn't so much the name itself as the way he said it…like a caress. She inwardly shuddered.

"No, thank you," Elenore whispered, scurrying off in the direction of the automatic doors.

The noonday sun beamed overhead, temporarily blinding her with its intensity.

She squinted against the brightness and hoisted the groceries up higher in her arms. She had a two mile walk ahead of her, and she needed to hurry if she thought to have dinner ready by the time her father arrived home.

The bags grew heavier the longer Elenore walked, until she thought for sure her arms would fall off.

A truck slowed to a stop beside her. "Need a lift?"

Elenore wanted to say yes, but of course, she didn't. Too many questions would be asked. She'd had her run-in with some of the town folk in the past, which only served to anger her father.

She shook her head and continued on.

"Suit yourself." The truck drove away.

Elenore arrived home approximately forty minutes after leaving the grocery store. Her feet ached almost as much as her arms did.

At least her father wasn't home. For that, she was grateful.

Since Elenore was no longer a minor, the state of Alabama had cut off any financial help Elijah had been receiving after his wife left him twelve years earlier.

He'd been forced to work on a more permanent basis, which afforded Elenore a daily reprieve from his presence. She loved being alone, with no one around but her animals.

Now that Elijah had a little money, he usually spent it on card games and prostitutes, which kept him busy more often than not.

Today would be a "not" day.

After putting the meager amount of groceries away, Elenore tied an apron around her waist and strode out to the chicken coop to gather the eggs.

She shooed the hens aside while attempting to dodge the piles of chicken droppings in her path. If not for the eggs and occasional meat the chickens provided, Elenore would go hungry.

Elijah left thirty dollars on the kitchen counter every Friday. Barely enough to buy the essentials, such as toilet paper and shampoo, let alone bread and canned foods.

So, Elenore had quickly learned how to budget…and shoplift anything she could fit in her pockets.

Once the eggs were gathered, she took out the chicken she'd killed the day before and started dinner.

Elenore had learned at an early age to shut down her emotions and do what had to be done. Besides, she told herself, killing a chicken was essential to her survival. *Nothing more.*

The old clapboard house she shared with her father quickly grew hot after turning on the oven. Even with the windows open, it became stifling. If not for the giant oak trees surrounding the house, she would probably be forced to cook outside.

Elenore wiped at her damp forehead with the back of her hand and switched on the television to watch the local news.

A pretty blonde anchorwoman sat behind a horseshoe-shaped desk, her red lipstick gleaming in the overhead lights. She spoke into the camera. *"Alan Brown makes the third person reported missing in the past two months. All three men are said to be from Haverty County, Alabama."*

Pictures appeared across the screen, with each man's name resting beneath.

Elenore wiped her hands on her apron and moved closer to the television.

"*Hector Gonzalez,*" the anchorwoman continued, "*was last seen nearly eight weeks ago at his place of employment. Dennis Baker went missing approximately a week later. And now, Alan Brown has disappeared. If you have seen or have information on the whereabouts of any of these men, we urge you to contact the Haverty County Sheriff's Department immediately.*"

The sound of a vehicle pulling up out front brought Elenore's head up. Her father was home.

She quickly switched off the television and hurried back to the kitchen to check on the biscuits.

His truck door slammed, filling Elenore with dread. There would be only one reason for his early arrival home… He'd been drinking.

He stomped his way up the back steps to the kitchen and threw open the door. "Elle!"

Elenore could smell the liquor on his breath long before he leaned down and spoke mere inches from her face. "How long before supper?"

She backed up a step. "I—It's almost ready."

His eyes narrowed, his gaze slowly lowering to her chest. "Good. That means we have time for a father-daughter talk."

Elenore swallowed her fear. "T-talk? What would you like to talk about, Daddy?"

"Take it off."

Nausea was instant. "I— The biscuits will burn."

"I don't give a crap about biscuits." He took a step forward, his hand going around to her backside. He squeezed it painfully before jerking her hard against his body. "Do what I said, girl."

Elenore's insides turned cold. There would be no stopping him, no talking him out of what he was about to do. She'd been through it enough times to know what would come next. What always came next.

He released her, spinning her around and shoving her toward the small kitchen table against the opposite wall.

The sound of his belt coming off could be heard over the thundering of her heart.

"Turn around," he slurred.

She couldn't face him for fear she would vomit on him.

He stepped in close behind her, pressing his disgusting erection against her backside. "Turn. Around."

The vomit she fought so hard to hold back shot to her throat, hovering there in the form of bile.

He grabbed a handful of her hair and jerked her head back, his wet, disgusting mouth hovering next to her ear. "You look just like your whore of a mama."

"D-Daddy, p-please," she whispered, knowing without question that begging would do no good. It never did any good.

He twisted her hair tightly in his hold and forced her forward until her face pressed hard against the tabletop.

His free hand yanked up the hem of her dress, tossing it upward around her shoulders.

Her underwear came down next, and then the sound of his sliding zipper echoed throughout the room with haunting finality.

Elenore gripped the edges of the table in preparation of the pain she knew would come.

She bit down on the inside of her lip to keep from crying out, her gaze locked onto the wall in front of her.

She forced her eyes to relax, the sound of the table scraping across the floor beneath her fading to the background. Her vision grew tunneled until her mind slipped into a place that shut out the pain and humiliation of his invasion. A place he couldn't follow. No one could follow…

Chapter Two

Elenore awoke the following morning, her entire body throbbing in pain.

She rolled over in bed to find the sun had already risen.

Panic quickly gripped her. Her father would be up soon, wanting his breakfast.

She tossed the covers back, wincing as she threw her legs over the side of the bed.

The tenderness at the juncture of her thighs was matched only by the pain in her shoulder.

Glancing down, she took in the bruising on her upper arm, the same arm her father had held behind her back as he… She shut down her thoughts, her mind unwilling to recall what had happened to her in that kitchen.

A knock sounded on her door.

Elenore righted her tattered nightgown and surged to her feet.

Her arms instinctively crossed over her chest in anticipation of Elijah's entry.

Odd that he knocked, she thought with more than a little fear, watching intently as the doorknob turned and Elijah stepped into the room.

He stood there, staring at the floor for long moments, and then he extended a cup in her direction. "Thought you might want some orange juice."

Confusion began to mingle with her fear as it always did. The man standing before her now was not the same man who had hurt her yesterday afternoon when he got home.

He took an awkward step forward, still holding that cup in his hand. "Go on, take it."

Elenore hesitantly moved toward him and accepted the cup of juice he held. He'd offered her his juice—a juice she wasn't normally allowed to touch.

He cleared his throat. "Look, Elle. I…um… I'm sorry about yesterday. You know how I get when I've been drinking. I would never hurt you for anything in the world."

More confusion settled in.

"I love you, Elle. I don't know what I would do if you left me like your mama did. I'll stop the drinking this time. I swear it."

Elenore's heart shifted. Her father loved her. That's all she'd ever wanted from him—his love and acceptance.

Part of her loved him in return. But a part, way down deep in her soul, hated the very ground he walked on.

Tears began to gather in her eyes. Maybe he meant it this time? Maybe he realized the monster he became when drinking, and he would finally quit?

She couldn't answer him, so great was the ache in her chest. She ached to be loved, ached to run away and never look back. But mostly, she ached for revenge.

How could she simply forgive him for the pain and humiliation she'd consistently endured at his hands? Hands that should show love and compassion. The very hands he held out to her now.

Elenore took deep, calming breaths, a coping mechanism she'd learned at an early age. She forced her mind to shut out the incomprehensible memories of the day before, set her juice on the nightstand, and moved on wooden legs into her father's outstretched arms.

He gently rocked her, murmuring soothing words above her head that made little sense. "You forgive your ole man?"

She nodded, more out of habit than consent.

"Good girl." He released her and took a step back. "Don't worry about making breakfast for me. I'm going fishing with Dale Mitchell this morning. I'll just grab something on the way."

Elenore stood rooted to the spot long after her father left the room.

Her emotions were all over the place. How could a man who was supposed to love her do the things he did to her? Was it her fault?

She'd come to the conclusion over the years that she was somehow to blame for her mother leaving. And that Mary Griffin's sudden departure was the sole reason her father drank like he did.

Elenore waited until she heard Elijah's truck leave the yard before she stumbled to the bathroom and vomited.

She retched so long and hard her stomach muscles screamed in protest. Yet no matter how much she heaved, she couldn't rid herself of his smell on her.

Staggering to her feet, she turned on the shower, stripped out of her well-worn gown, and stepped under the spray.

She would scrub herself until she bled, if that's what it took to feel clean. But Elenore would never feel clean again. Never.

After her shower, she took down a green dress that had seen better days. But the sleeves were short and the material thin. Which seemed practical given the sweltering heat that was sure to arrive.

She would give anything for a pair of jeans, or pants of any kind, for that matter. But Elijah refused to let her have them. He claimed they were of the devil and reserved for men and… whores.

Slipping on the dress, she moved to stand in front of her mirror. She pulled her long blonde hair back into a ponytail and stared at her reflection. She really did resemble her mother.

Resentment boiled up inside her, the longer she stood there, looking at herself. *That is what Daddy sees when he looks at me,* she thought with more than a little disgust. *Mother.*

An image of Mary Griffin's crying face suddenly flashed through Elenore's mind. *"Elijah, don't!"*

A whimper escaped Elenore. She staggered back a few steps, her hand flying to her mouth.

The memory of Mary trying desperately to protect her daughter didn't add up with the tales Elenore had been told all her life. Even though the stories came from Elijah, Elenore had no reason not to believe him. Why else would her mother have left her behind?

According to Elijah, Mary had run off with a friend of his when Elenore was eight years old.

She'd never returned or attempted to contact her daughter in the last twelve years.

Elenore hated herself in that moment more than she'd ever hated herself before. Something was wrong with her, something bad enough that her own mother hadn't wanted her. And though her father had never walked away from her, he blamed her for her mother leaving. Elenore could see it in his eyes. Especially when he drank.

Chapter Three

Evan Ramirez entered Gerald's Diner at nine a.m., approximately twenty minutes after his meeting with Sheriff Donnie King.

The sheriff had wanted to personally congratulate Evan on his recent move to their fine town, not to mention being Haverty County's new investigator. He'd also handed Evan his first official case.

"Mornin', Detective." Minnie Anderson greeted Evan as he took a seat near the window. "Will you be having breakfast?"

Evan shook his head, sending Minnie a friendly smile. In the few short weeks he'd been in Wexler, she'd taken exceptionally good care of him. "Just coffee, please."

As far as waitresses went, Minnie Anderson was a good one. She treated all her customers equally and never forgot a face. Her memory was as sharp as a tack, even though she had to be pushing eighty years old.

She bustled over and set a cup of black coffee in front of Evan. "Any news on Selma's husband?"

Selma's husband happened to be Hector Gonzalez, the first man to go missing from Wexler.

"Nothing yet," Evan admitted after taking a sip of his coffee. "I was just handed the case this morning. Hopefully, we know something soon."

Mabel Jenkins, who sat at the end of the bar, piped in. "The first place I'd be checking, if it were me, would be over at the Griffin's. Hector Gonzalez worked at the lumber yard with Elijah Griffin, from what I understand. Matter of fact, according to Hector's wife, she ran Elijah off from her house about a week before Hector came up missing. She said Elijah had shown up there drunk, demanding Hector pay him some money he owed him."

"Mabel!" Minnie quickly scolded. "It ain't very Christian-like to talk about folks behind their back."

The one known as Mabel sent Minnie a go-to the devil look. "I never claimed to a be a Christian. Besides, I reckon Jesus knows what Elijah Griffin is all about, as well as the rest of us do."

Evan cleared his throat. "Be that as it may, Miss Jenkins, it doesn't mean that Mr. Griffin had anything to do with Hector's disappearance."

"Name's Mabel," she shot back with a side glance. "Miss Jenkins was my grandma."

Evan fought a laugh. "I'm sorry, Mabel. It won't happen again."

The bell above the door chimed, announcing the appearance of Deputy Charlie Taylor.

He removed his hat, the bald spot on his head shining under the florescent lights.

"Morning, Charlie," the entire diner chorused as the deputy made his way over to Evan's table.

Charlie tipped his head to the room at large, adjusted his gun belt beneath his overly big belly, and took a seat across from Evan. "It's south of Hades out there already. I thought for sure I'd die of heat stroke when I got out of my car. Does it get this hot in Mexico?"

A muscle ticked along Evan's jaw. "I wouldn't know. I'm from Georgia."

"Oh." Genuine embarrassment shone from Charlie's eyes. "I just assumed with your name being Ramirez…"

"I was born in Atlanta." Evan decided to change the subject. "What can you tell me about the three missing men from Wexler?"

Charlie blew out a breath, moving his hands out of the way as Minnie set his coffee in front of him. "All three had arrest records. Everything from DUIs to domestic disputes. Why, what are you thinking?"

Evan shrugged. "I don't know yet. We had a similar case in Atlanta, involving the disappearance of four women."

"Were any of them ever located?" Charlie picked up his coffee and blew into the cup.

"Yes. They'd all been murdered by the same man."

Charlie nearly choked on his coffee. "Murdered? Did you find the guy?"

"We did. But the women had something in common… They worked the street corners. And this particular killer had a fetish for young prostitutes. It became his downfall. He was eventually picked up for soliciting an undercover. At which point we matched his DNA with one of the victims we had found earlier in the year. He told us where to find the other three women in exchange for avoiding the electric chair."

Minnie meandered over and placed a plate of food in front of Charlie, even though Evan hadn't heard him order.

Charlie plucked up the salt and began shaking it vigorously over his sunny-side-up eggs. He paused, meeting Evan's gaze. "Give her another week, and Minnie will have you figured out. I haven't placed an order here in probably ten years. She knows what I'm having before I do."

Evan shook his head at the enormous amount of food on Charlie's plate.

"He's a growing boy," Minnie announced with a wink and a pat to Charlie's back. "Besides, we've grown rather fond of him over the years."

Charlie smiled but continued doctoring up his food.

Once the waitress wandered off, Evan pinned Charlie with a serious look. "Tell me about Elijah Griffin."

Taking a rather large bite of his eggs, Charlie appeared thoughtful. He spoke around his mouthful of food. "He's the town drunk. Or used to be until he got that last DUI. Now, he gets others to drive him around when he's been drinking. At least that's what I hear, anyway. It's been a while since I've had to lock him up."

Mabel spoke up once again. "He needs to be in prison for what he's done to that girl."

Evan shifted his focus to Mabel. "What did he do and to whom?"

The older woman slid off her stool and trailed over to stand next to Evan's table. "That girl of his. His daughter. He's been beating on her since the day she screamed her way into this world."

"Now, Mabel," Charlie interjected, half turning in his seat to face her. "That's pure gossip. We don't have any evidence to back that up."

Mabel narrowed her eyes in Charlie's direction. "Don't we? Why don't you ask Claire Lewis how much evidence she had against Elijah? If not for that old geezer Judge Powell turning a blind eye, it would have been three hots and a cot for Elijah Griffin."

Evan pulled a twenty-dollar bill from his pocket and dropped it onto the table. He nodded to Charlie and then stood. "Breakfast is on me."

"Where are you off to in such a hurry?" Charlie plucked up the money. "Appreciate that."

"I've got something to do here in town first, then I'm going to drive out to Elijah Griffin's place and have a chat with him."

Charlie picked up a napkin and wiped at his mouth. "Want me to ride with?"

"That's all right, Charlie. Finish your breakfast. I'm just going to ask him a couple of questions."

Turning on his heel, Evan sent Minnie a wink and strolled out the door.

Chapter Four

Elenore dropped her head back on her shoulders while rolling it from side to side. Milking the cow had never been an easy chore, but to do it in the dead of summer made it twice as hard.

It didn't help that her body ached in places it shouldn't, and it hurt to sit on the small wooden seat of the stool beneath her.

Pushing to her feet, Elenore nearly lost her balance. She was more than a little grateful when she didn't spill the pail of milk she'd work so hard for.

After taking the milk to kitchen, Elenore returned to the rundown barn out back and untied the cow. She then made her way to the chicken coop to check for eggs.

The coop wasn't in much better shape than the barn, but it sat beneath a cluster of oak trees, affording the chickens a cool, shaded area to scratch around in.

"Move aside," Elenore announced, entering the coop. "Y'all know the drill."

She leaned down to gather some eggs from a laying box, when an image of the missing man from television flashed through her mind. *Hector Gonzalez.*

Hector had visited Elenore shortly before his disappearance. As had Dennis Baker and Alan Brown.

Elijah had been selling Elenore to a few of the men in town since she'd been a young girl. He would allow them an hour with her, to do with what they wanted, no matter how vile or cruel. And some of them were exceptionally cruel.

The sound of a vehicle coming up the dirt drive caught Elenore off guard.

She quickly gathered up the rest of the eggs, tucked them into her apron, and left the coop.

There, slowing to a stop not twenty feet in front of her, was a Haverty County patrol car.

Shielding her eyes against the midmorning sun, Elenore anxiously watched a tall, dark-haired man exit the vehicle.

"Is this the Griffin place?" the officer called out in a clear, deep voice.

Elenore wanted to run inside. She had dealt with the police before, years ago after the Department of Children and Families had been called on Elijah.

If her father returned home to find a deputy in the yard, Elenore would suffer the consequences.

She averted her gaze. "Yes, it is."

The office advanced, his steps sure and precise. "I need to speak with Elijah Griffin. Is he around?"

Elenore shook her head. "He's not here."

"My name's Evan Ramirez. I'm an investigator with the Haverty County Sheriff's Department."

Elenore nodded her understanding but kept her gaze on a tree to his left.

"And you are?" he prompted, placing his body in her line of sight.

She swallowed down her panic and met his gaze. He had kind, green eyes. There was nothing lascivious lurking in their depths. She relaxed a little. Very little.

"Elenore. Elenore Griffin. Like I said, my daddy's not here."

He nodded toward her arm, his demeanor suddenly changing. "Are you all right?"

Elenore immediately covered the bruise he referred to with her hand. "I'm fine. Fell in the barn, is all."

He didn't believe her, if his expression were any indication. "Are you sure you're okay? That's a pretty bad bruise you have there. Have you had it looked at?"

Elenore cleared her throat and backed up a step. "Really, I'm fine, Mr. Ramirez. I need to finish the chores. But I'll let Daddy know you stopped by."

He nodded, reaching into his shirt pocket and pulling out a business card. "I appreciate that, Elenore." He held it out to her.

It wasn't lost on her that he kept his stance nonthreatening while extending the card toward her. He was obviously trying not to frighten her.

She relaxed a little more and accepted the card. "I don't know when he'll be home, but I'll see that he gets this."

He glanced at her feet, his gaze softening even more.

Embarrassment was swift. She knew her shoes were stained, and a hole was present on the side of one. She was also hyperaware of how dirty her legs and hands were. But working among chickens, pigs, and cows would do that to a person.

As uncomfortable as Elenore felt under his perusal, it was nothing compared to the anxiety she experienced over her father coming home to find her talking to the police.

Evan Ramirez must have sensed her inner conflict. He turned to go. But not before his gaze touched on everything from the barn to the house. "I'll check back later."

Elenore stood rooted to the spot while he sauntered back to his car and slid behind the wheel.

He backed out of the dirt drive, leaving her to wonder what the police wanted with her father.

Yeah, Elijah wouldn't be happy about it all.

She crumpled the card into a little ball in her palm, dug a small hole in the dirt at her feet, and buried it.

Chapter Five

Evan drove away from the Griffin place with his stomach in knots.

He had seen more domestic violence and child abuse in his five years with the Atlanta Police Department than he cared to remember. He knew the signs. And there were definitely red flags flying all over the place he'd just left.

The bruising on Elenore Griffin's arm didn't come from an accident in the barn. The distinct outline of fingerprints marred her skin.

But there was nothing Evan could do. She hadn't filed a report that he was aware of. And according to her records, she was a grown woman. Twenty years old to be exact.

Why would a twenty-year-old still live at home with a father that obviously abused her? he wondered, turning onto the main road.

It wasn't as if she didn't have options. Haverty County might be small, but they did have a shelter.

Evan ran a hand down his face, unable to remove the image of Elenore Griffin from his mind.

She had dark blonde hair. The kind most folks referred to as dirty blonde or dishwater blonde. Her eyes were a crystal blue, bright and stunning in their brilliance. She wore no makeup, and smudges of what he'd assumed to be dirt had streaked the side of her face.

She'd worn a dingy, green dress that fell below her knees, and her shoes were tattered and worn. She was thin…too thin.

Evan had just witnessed an obvious case of mental and physical abuse. And it angered him.

He would never understand how a man could put his hands on a woman, period. Let alone his own daughter.

And as so many others like her, Elenore wouldn't leave. Whether from fear or mental dependency, Evan wasn't sure.

Something about Elenore had moved him. Protective instincts he forgot he had stirred to life inside him. He wanted to save her, even though he doubted he could.

His stomach picked that moment to growl. He hadn't had anything but coffee since the night before.

He pulled into a parking space in front of Gerald's Diner and switched off the engine. But he couldn't seem get out. He was about to go inside and order while that poor girl he'd just left worked outside in the heat, probably hungry.

"Christ," he sighed, opening his car door. Legally, he could do absolutely zilch for that girl.

"Back so soon?" Minnie greeted him with a friendly smile as Evan stepped inside the diner. "You should have had breakfast. It's the most important meal of the day."

Evan returned her smile and took his previous seat at the window. "You're right, Minnie. What's the special today?"

She rattled off something about meatloaf and mashed potatoes.

"I'll have that," he muttered, glancing at Mabel still sitting at the bar.

He wondered briefly if she had been there all morning or if, like him, she'd returned for lunch. Either way, she seemed to be a wealth of information about the goings-on in Wexler, and he intended to pick her brain.

Making a decision, he got up and wandered over to the bar to stand at her elbow. "Mabel."

She sent him a nod but didn't look up at him. "Detective."

Evan thought his words over carefully. "Earlier, you mentioned some things about Elijah Griffin and his daughter. Do you know them personally?"

She shook her head. "I knew his wife, Mary. Nice woman. Pretty too. But she supposedly ran off with a friend of his and hasn't been seen since. It's a shame she didn't take that girl with her."

Evan pulled a stool out and took a seat. "How old was the child when Mary Griffin left?"

Mabel appeared thoughtful for a moment. "I reckon she was around seven or eight. Just a little thing. Makes no sense why her mama would abandon her. She seemed pretty taken with her."

"And you think Elijah is abusing his daughter?" Evan intentionally left out Elenore's name to avoid unwanted questions.

Mabel lifted her head and met his gaze. "I would stake my farm on it. You need to go talk to Claire Lewis. She works for the local Department of Children and Families. Been there for nigh of twenty years now. She worked the Griffin case until that moron judge threw it out. She'll have more answers than I do."

Evan touched Mabel on the arm. "Thank you, Miss—I mean, Mabel. I appreciate you speaking with me."

He got up to head back to his table, but her next words stopped him. "Get her out of that place, Detective. Before he kills her."

Mabel's words echoed inside Evan's mind as he made his way back to his table.

He took a seat, not surprised to see a cup of black coffee steaming up in front of him.

"Thank you, Minnie." He took a small sip, careful not to burn his tongue.

Minnie bustled over, carrying his food. She placed the plate in front of him. "I'm not a gossip, Detective, but I've heard stories about that poor girl out at the Griffin place. Might be worth looking into."

Evan picked up his fork. "Do you know where the DCF office is in town?"

"Department of Children and Families?"

At his nod, she continued. "Right across the street."

Evan swung his gaze to the window he sat next to and studied the various offices in the vicinity.

"It's the one with the green and gold sign above it," Minnie told him, tapping a bony finger on the window. "You can't miss it. It's right next to the pharmacy."

Evan thanked her and dove into his lunch. The meatloaf had to be the best he'd ever tasted.

He ate with a vengeance and then paid his bill and left.

Leaving his car parked at the diner, Evan jogged across the street and opened the door to the DCF office.

A young brunette sat behind a desk, stamping a stack of papers.

She looked up when Evan approached. "May I help you?"

"I'm looking for Claire Lewis. Is she in?"

The brunette nodded. "She is. If you'll have a seat, I'll let her know that you're here."

"Thank you." Evan moved toward a row of chairs to the left of the front door.

"Can I get your name?"

"Detective Ramirez," he immediately answered.

With nod, the brunette picked up the phone and spoke low into the receiver before hanging up. "She'll be right with you, Detective."

Evan waited for probably ten minutes, then an older woman rounded the corner, holding a clipboard in her hands. "Mr. Ramirez?"

"Yes, ma'am." Evan stood.

She waved him forward. "Right this way."

Evan followed the woman down a short hallway and into a small office adorned with several large filing cabinets, a desk, and two folding chairs.

"Have a seat, Detective. What can I help you with?"

Evan parked it in one of the metal chairs. "Thank you, Mrs. Lewis. I'm investigating a case involving three missing gentlemen from Haverty County. And I was wondering if you could give me some insight into Elijah Griffin."

The older woman's eyes narrowed behind her glasses. "Is he suspected of being involved somehow?"

Evan shook his head. "No, ma'am. He's simply a person of interest. I'd like as much information as I can get before I speak with him."

Claire Lewis leaned back in her chair and pinned Evan with a serious look. "Elijah Griffin is one of the evilest beings I have ever run across."

She pushed to her feet and turned to pull open a drawer on one of the tall filing cabinets behind her.

Evan watched her shut that drawer and open another one.

She dug around in the cabinet for a couple more minutes before pulling a thick file from its depths. Which, she dropped heavily in front of Evan. "Here you go. This is everything I have on that monster."

Evan opened the folder to find a picture of a young girl, about eight years old, with bruising on the side of her face and her left arm in a cast.

His stomach tightened. "Her father did this?"

"He did a heck of a lot more than that. Keep looking."

Taking a fortifying breath, Evan turned to the next page and read the doctor's report from the first picture.

Eight-year-old female presents with multiple injuries.

Evan continued to read, noticing the words *concussion, trauma,* and *broken bones.* And then his gaze landed on *vaginal penetration.*

He looked up at Claire Lewis in horror. "He raped his own daughter?"

"More than once," she admitted, nodding toward the folder. "We were able to remove little Elenore from the home and place her in foster care. But when it came time to go to court with the case, the judge sent her right back into that hellhole."

Evan couldn't believe what he heard. "How—? Why?"

Claire shrugged. "He claimed we didn't have sufficient evidence to convict her father. Threw the case out on some technicality."

Evan rubbed at the back of his neck, Elenore's crystal-blue eyes haunting him. "But as she got older, she could have testified or—"

"She wouldn't," Clair interrupted, removing her glasses. "We know that abuse or neglect of children is tragically common in our society. We're not even surprised when studies point to a strong link between the physical, sexual, or psychological mistreatment of children and the development of psychiatric problems."

She took a deep breath and leaned forward, resting her elbows on the desktop. "A lot of mental health professionals resort to personality theories. Maybe a child's protective mechanisms become self-defeating when they become adults."

Claire opened a drawer and pulled out some papers that were stapled together. "In this article it's said that there's a strong indication that childhood abuse causes serious psychosocial development, leaving a wounded child within the adult they become. It's similar to Stockholm syndrome."

Evan continued looking through the photos of Elenore Griffin at different stages in her life…different injuries and ages. "The psychological damage done to her…"

"Yes," Claire quietly stated. "In all likelihood, Elenore Griffin may be too far gone to reach."

Evan opened his mouth to argue, but Claire held up a hand, stopping him. "I worked that girl's case for years, Detective. *Years.* Everything that could have been done was done to save her. Until she grew to be a teenager and stopped cooperating. Whether from fear or some other reason we may never fully understand, I don't know. But I can tell you this, if you can find evidence to put that sorry father of hers away, there just might be a small chance that she can come back from the nightmare she's known all her life."

"Do you mind if I take this?" Evan indicated the folder in front of him, as well as the article Claire had taken from the drawer.

Claire plucked up the article and slipped it inside the folder. "I'll get Daphne to make you copies of everything. It won't take that long."

Evan nodded. "Thank you, Mrs. Lewis. I appreciate all your help."

Claire gathered up the folder and left the room, leaving Evan to sit there, reeling from everything he'd learned. Elenore Griffin had lived through a nightmare that most could never imagine. A nightmare he intended to save her from.

Chapter Six

Elenore awoke the following morning, relieved to realize her father hadn't come home the night before.

Of course, that meant he was probably drinking and would likely return home drunk or severely hungover. Either way, it didn't bode well for her.

She rolled out of bed and dressed in an off-white, floral print dress.

Pulling her hair back into a ponytail, she slipped on her shoes, only to discover her foot had busted through the side of one.

The ripped material had finally given way. Which meant, she had no shoes to wear.

Removing the shoe, she hobbled through the house and outside to the old shed that sat behind the chicken coop, in search of some duct tape.

Holding the torn shoe in her hand, she rounded the coop and lost her footing in a pile of soft dirt. She wound up face-first in the black Alabama soil.

Lifting her head, Elenore spat several times before pushing to her feet. She'd skinned one of her knees as well as the palm of her left hand.

The fall itself had been painful, jarring the previous injuries she'd sustained from her father.

And speaking of her father, she'd better hurry before he came home and caught her snooping through his shed.

Elenore gritted her teeth, picked up her tattered shoe, and limped the rest of the way to the shed.

Odd, the door wasn't closed all the way, she thought, pulling it fully open.

The first thing she noticed was a shovel lying on the floor. Black dirt covered the blade of it.

Her father must have used it and forgot to put it up.

Elenore picked up the shovel, wincing at the scrape on her palm, and then hung it back in its usual spot on a rack along the wall.

She then grabbed the duct tape and made quick work of her torn shoe. She put the tape back and slipped her foot into the hideous thing.

With a sigh, she left the shed and limped her way back toward the house to clean up her injuries.

The sound of a vehicle coming up the drive brought her up short. She turned in time to see Detective Ramirez come to a stop and exit his car.

He hurried in her direction. "Miss Griffin, are you all right?"

Elenore stumbled back, her gaze darting to the house, half expecting her father to come barreling out the back door. "I-I'm fine."

"You don't look fine," he rushed out, dropping to his haunches in front of her. "You're hurt."

She wanted to crawl in a hole and die. He was practically on his knees, his face a mere two feet from her duct-taped shoe. "It's just a skinned knee. I was about to go inside and clean it up."

He rose to his full height, which in her estimation was probably somewhere in the vicinity of six-feet-two. "Here, let me help you."

Horrified that he would attempt to go inside the house, Elenore shook her head while backing up another step. "I-I can take care of it on my own. You're making a fuss out of nothing."

"I'm not fussing. I just want to help." He took hold of her elbow and guided her toward the back steps.

There was nothing shy of shoving him back that she could do to sway him from following her inside.

More embarrassment flooded her.

Though the house was clean enough to eat off the floors, it was old and severely outdated. And Elijah had never installed air conditioning, so the place felt like an oven.

Elenore hobbled up the steps, her stomach a ball of nerves, knowing the detective was tight on her heels.

He didn't speak as he stepped inside the overly warm kitchen and pulled out a chair from the small table against the wall. The same table Elijah had recently…hurt her on.

"Where can I find a washcloth?"

Elenore nodded toward the sink. "Under there."

Evan spun toward the sink, opening the cabinets directly below it. He snagged a white washcloth and then looked back at her. "Where's the peroxide?"

Growing more nervous by the second, Elenore shook her head. Elijah could drive up any second now. "We don't have anything like that here. Please, Detective, I don't like to be fussed over."

"Nonsense." He sent her a reassuring smile. "Who needs peroxide, anyway? Good old-fashioned soap and water should do the trick."

Evan straightened and turned on the faucet. Once he soaped up the washcloth, he rinsed it a little and moved to hunker down in front of her. "This may sting some."

He dabbed around the scrape and then gently cleansed it, glancing at the duct tape on her shoe.

"May I?" He nodded toward her battered footwear.

She removed the shoe, holding perfectly still while he set about cleaning her up.

"What size shoe do you wear?"

Elenore didn't flinch. She'd had way worse injuries than a minor scrape. "Why?"

Evan shrugged. "Just curious."

"A seven. But I don't see why that matters."

"There. All done," he announced, ignoring her words.

A door slammed outside, sending Elenore shooting to her feet. "Daddy's home!"

Evan shot her an odd look before returning to the sink to rinse out the bloodied washcloth.

Elenore had never felt so sick in all her life. Elijah was going to walk through that back door at any second and find the detective standing in his kitchen.

"Elle!" The door swung open with enough force it knocked a picture off the wall behind it. "What in God's name is the law doing here?"

Elenore's voice stuck in her throat.

Evan calmly wiped his hands on his pants and leaned his hip against the counter. "Elijah Griffin?"

"Who are you, and what are you doing in my house?"

"I'm Detective Ramirez. Your daughter hurt herself, and I simply assisted her inside."

Elijah stomped forward, his seething gaze touching on Elenore before settling on the detective once more. "You've done your good deed for the day. Now, you can get your behind out of my house."

"Actually, I came here looking for you," Evan continued as if Elijah hadn't just ordered him to leave.

Which only angered Elijah even more.

"Looking for me, for what?"

"If you wouldn't mind coming in to answer a few questions, I—"

Elijah barked out a laugh, effectively cutting off the rest of the detective's words. "Get your sorry behind out of my house. I ain't going anywhere with you."

Elenore kept her head down, half expecting her father to strike her in front of the detective.

The sound of Evan's shoes thumping on the floor could be heard over the thundering of Elenore's heart.

She didn't want him to leave because leaving meant she would suffer the wrath of Elijah.

The door clicking shut behind the detective sounded overly loud in the otherwise quiet room.

Elijah didn't move until the detective's car could no longer be heard leaving the driveway.

"Get in your room."

"Daddy, please! I didn't invite him here. He just—"

"I said go to your room!"

She bumped into the chair she'd been sitting in earlier, nearly toppling it over behind her.

"And get out of that dress," he yelled as she rounded the corner to her small bedroom.

Tears of terror began to gather in her eyes. Her entire body shook with fear. Fear of what he would do, fear of how badly he would hurt her this time. But mostly she feared that she would survive to endure another day.

Elenore removed her clothes and then sat on the edge of her bed as she knew Elijah would expect her to do.

The sound of the back door opening and closing again reached her ears, seconds before a man holding a briefcase stepped inside her room.

Elenore recognized him instantly. Terror unlike anything her father had made her feel consumed her. She had experienced Bill too many times to remember.

Elijah stood behind him, staring into Elenore's eyes from over the man's shoulder. "Don't disappoint him if you know what's good for you. I'll be back in an hour." He turned and left the room, closing the door behind him.

Elenore crossed her arms over her chest, her panic and horror choking her. She couldn't breathe, couldn't think.

Bill set his briefcase down and stripped out of his clothes. "You know the drill. Lie down on the bed. Face-down."

She watched in horror as he opened the briefcase and removed a strap, some rope, and something that looked like a baton the police normally used.

He held up the baton for her to see. "Do you remember this? No? You'll be reacquainted before you know it. Don't worry, I brought lube."

Her teeth began to chatter. "P-please, don't do this."

His answer was to stride across the floor and backhand her to her back. He then flipped her to her stomach and set about tying her hands and feet to the corner posts of her bed.

Elenore screamed, fighting in earnest. But she was no match for the man called Bill.

Chapter Seven

A week had passed since Evan's visit to the Griffin place. He'd wanted to return a dozen times, but without evidence of foul play, Elijah Griffin could file charges of harassment.

A light tap on his office door alerted him to Sheriff Donnie King's presence.

The sheriff poked his head inside. "Busy?"

"Come on in, Sheriff. I was just going over the missing persons cases."

Donnie stepped into the room and took a seat in the chair in front of Evan's desk. "Having any luck?"

Evan shook his head. "Dennis Baker's wife is pretty distraught, though. They have four children together and one from a previous marriage. I don't know what she's going to do. She doesn't work."

The sheriff ran a hand through his graying hair. "She needs to contact Claire Lewis over at the Department of Children and Families. She should be able to point Mrs. Baker in the right direction for public assistance."

"I'll call Mrs. Baker this morning and let her know."

"What about the families of the other two missing?" the sheriff questioned.

Evan opened the file in front of him. "Hector Gonzalez's wife works at a clothing store in town. Their house is paid for. She seems to be making it all right. As for Mrs. Brown, I haven't been able to catch her home long enough to speak with her."

Scanning Alan Brown's file, Evan murmured, "It looks like William Burnham spoke with Mrs. Brown about Elijah Griffin on several different occasions before he retired but learned nothing notable from her. She has no children or family in town."

Donnie nodded. "William was a very good investigator. If there was something off with the wife, he definitely would have noted it."

Evan had only met William Burnham once or twice before taking over the man's job. Burnham had retired from the Haverty County Sheriff's Office as the only investigator the department had. Of course, with only two thousand four hundred and fifteen souls living in Haverty County, the department hadn't needed more than one.

"How did it go with Elijah Griffin?" Donnie sat forward, resting his forearms on his knees.

Evan barked out a humorless laugh. "Not good. To say he was enraged about my arrival at his place would be an understatement. He ran me off the second he pulled up."

"Oh, you arrived ahead of him?"

"Yes." Evan glanced down at the picture of Elenore resting in the folder in front of him. "His daughter had hurt herself. I helped her into the house and cleaned up her wound. Her father pulled up while I was in the kitchen, tending to her."

Donnie whistled through his teeth. "It's a wonder you didn't get shot. Elijah Griffin is a mean son of a gun who happened to beat the system at every turn. It ticks me off to no end."

Evan lifted his gaze. "Beat the system?"

"On more than one occasion."

Leaning back in his chair, Evan crossed his arms over his chest. "I read about the case with his daughter. How it was thrown out of court, and he resumed custody of her."

Donnie's gaze grew distant. "That poor girl. The entire town was in an uproar over that. But that was just the beginning. She's been in the local emergency room more times than I can count. But she always defended him, maintaining that she fell or was injured by one of the animals out there on that farm."

Evan's brow furrowed. "I spoke with Claire Lewis about Elenore. Claire believes the girl suffers from something similar to Stockholm syndrome."

"Stockholm syndrome is something that abductees experience toward their captors. Elenore isn't an abductee," the sheriff pointed out.

"I know." Evan went on to fill Donnie in on his discussion with Claire, ending with, "I believe he's broken her. I think he has such control over her that she lives in a bubble, where nothing and no one exists in her mind but him. Sure, she fears him. That's the weapon he uses to keep that control."

Donnie nodded. "You're probably right about that. What's your gut telling you? Do you think Elijah Griffin had something to do with the disappearances?"

"I do. And I aim to prove it. In fact, I'm heading back out there this morning to question him about Hector Gonzalez. Not only did they work together, but according to Hector's wife, she had to run him off not long before Hector disappeared. Apparently, Elijah had shown up over there drunk, demanding some money that Hector owed him."

"That doesn't mean Elijah is responsible for Hector's disappearance," Donnie cautioned.

"You're right, Sheriff. But it's a place to start."

The sheriff got to his feet. "Just be careful out there. Elijah Griffin is a dangerous man. God only knows what he'll resort to if he feels cornered. The man thinks he's above the law."

"Speaking of being above the law." Evan stood too. "I'm going to question Judge Powell, too. As soon as I get back from the Griffin place."

Donnie's eyebrows shot up. "Question him about?"

"Elenore Griffin."

"You're playing with fire, Evan. That case was tried years ago. Which means that no matter what you dig up on Elijah Griffin, that verdict can never be overturned."

Evan was all too aware. "Yes, sir. I understand that. But something is off about this entire scenario. Something that goes deeper than a missing persons case."

"What are you thinking?" The sheriff's demeanor never changed.

That was one of the things Evan liked about Donnie King. He remained open-minded, didn't interfere with Evan's methods, and genuinely cared about his town.

Evan took a deep breath. "I don't think Gonzalez, Brown, and Baker are missing... I think they were murdered."

Chapter Eight

Elenore left the grocery store with more items than she'd purchased the week before.

Her father had left fifty dollars on the counter for groceries this time. That was twenty more than the usual thirty he normally left every week. Which meant that he obviously felt guilty about leaving her alone with Bill.

She hoisted the bags higher up in her arms and began the long trek down the clay road toward home.

Elenore's injuries left by Bill had mostly healed. The things he'd done to her while she'd been tied face-down on that bed, were cruel and inhumane.

Elijah had shown remorse when he'd come home to find her still restrained and bleeding from every orifice in her body.

He had gently untied her and carried her to the shower. He obviously hadn't known how badly Bill would hurt her, or he would never have left her there alone with him. At least that's what Elenore told herself.

Elijah loved her. Even though he didn't always show it. She knew he cared about her. At least when he was sober.

She tried to steer clear of her father when he'd been drinking. Nothing good ever came of it. He usually ended up angry...and the blame always landed at her feet.

Yet he hadn't been drinking when he'd left her alone with Bill, her mind whispered. But she pushed the thought back.

Slivers of sand from the clay road made its way past the duct tape and into Elenore's shoe. It ground beneath her toes, to scrub along the bottom of her foot.

She wanted to stop and clear the sand free, but that would mean setting the groceries down to do it. And she'd never be able to hoist all three bags back into her arms without help.

The sound of a vehicle coming up the road behind her sent Elenore moving to the right as far as the road would allow without sending her to the ditch.

She kept her head down and her feet moving forward.

The car stopped. "Elenore?"

Her head came up at the sound of Evan's voice.

He leaned across the seat and threw the passenger side door open. "Get in."

"I can walk, Detective."

He simply sat there, unmoving. "I was headed to your house, anyway. Get in, Elenore. I'm not going to leave you out here to walk in this heat."

Without giving her a chance to decline his offer once more, Evan got out of the car, rounded the back, and took two of the bags from her arms. He placed them in the back seat.

Elenore had to admit, it felt so very good to have the heavy weight gone from her screaming shoulders.

Evan shut the back door and opened the front. "Please, get in."

After another brief hesitation, Elenore did as he asked.

He slid back behind the wheel, turned up the air conditioning, and then leaned across her to grab hold of her seatbelt.

"Watch the bag," he murmured, finagling the seatbelt between her and the groceries she held.

Once he had her buckled in, he put the car in drive and carefully maneuvered down the washboard-riddled clay road. "Why are you walking in this heat, carrying three bags of groceries?"

Elenore didn't know how to respond. So she kept quiet.

But Evan wouldn't let it go. "I mean, isn't there someone who could give you a ride into town?"

Elenore shook her head. She had no one. No family, no friends. The closest person she had to a friend was the mailman, Clarence Price.

Clarence had always been nice to Elenore. When she was younger, he would often bring her a piece of candy when he had to deliver mail to them. Until Elijah caught him doing it and nearly cost Clarence his job.

Clarence still smiled and waved at Elenore when he'd catch her outside, but he never brought candy with him anymore.

"There is no one," she whispered, unable to look at the detective.

He blew out an exhausted-sounding sigh. "I gave you my card, Elenore. Next time you need to go to town for anything, call me. I don't mind giving you a ride."

She wanted to tell him that Elijah would likely bury him beneath the chicken coop, but she refrained.

"I brought you something," Evan continued as if she hadn't ignored his last statement.

That brought her head around. "Me?"

His smile, though genuine, held a hint of nervousness in it. As if being insecure wasn't a feeling he was accustomed to. "In the box, on the seat."

Elenore's gaze lowered to that box against her will. Aside from the mailman who used to bring her candy on occasion, no one had ever bought her a gift.

She stared at that box with a longing that left an ache in her chest.

"Go on," Evan insisted in a soft voice. "It's not much, but…"

Elenore glanced at him before returning her gaze to the box. "What is it?"

"Open it and see." He laughed, a sound that seemed natural coming from him.

Shifting the groceries on her lap, Elenore slowly reached for the gray box resting between them.

She realized her fingers slightly shook as she carefully lifted the lid.

Inside were a pair of running shoes equipped with memory foam and pink stripes along the sides.

Elenore's breath caught. She'd never owned a pair of expensive shoes before.

"Try them on. See how they feel."

She wanted to. God, did she ever want to.

But then, reality settled over her in a blanket of sorrow. Her father would never allow her to keep them. In fact, he would likely punish her for accepting them. And God only knew what he would do to Evan. "I can't."

"Sure, you can."

She shook her head. "Daddy would never."

"So, don't tell him."

Her gaze flew to Evan's face. "He would know. He would find out."

All too soon, they were pulling into Elenore's drive. Thankfully, her father wasn't home.

Evan appeared to consider her words. "You're twenty years old, Elenore. Your father can't tell you what shoes you can and can't have."

The detective would never understand, Elenore decided, reaching for the door handle.

"Wait." Evan replaced the lid on the box. "How about you tell him that you found them at the thrift store for three dollars?"

Elenore thought about the extra money her father had given her after Bill's departure. She could probably convince him that she'd bought the shoes at a secondhand store.

Evan took the shoes from the box, removed the tags, and handed them to her. "I'll keep the box."

Without waiting to see if she accepted the gift, he got out and unloaded the groceries from the back.

Elenore picked up the shoes and brought them to her nose. She had fallen in love with that new smell when she'd been in foster care, and one of her foster moms had purchased her a new pair of sandals.

Making a decision, she dropped the shoes into the grocery bag and followed Evan to the back door of the house. "You can just leave the groceries on the steps, Detective."

He looked as if he would argue but then decided against it.

With a nod, he did as she asked. "I need to speak with your father. Do you know when he'll be home?"

Elenore's heartbeat kicked up a notch. "What do you need to talk to Daddy about?"

Evan's head tilted to the side. "Are you afraid of him, Elenore?"

Realizing she'd need to be more careful around the detective, Elenore shook her head. "I'm not. I just don't like seeing him upset, is all."

The detective didn't appear to buy her explanation, but he didn't push. "In that case, I'll just wait for him."

Elenore's stomach dropped. Her mind began to scramble for explanations as to why Evan couldn't hang around and wait for Elijah. "He's out of town."

Evan's eyes narrowed. "He's out of town. Really?"

Elenore nodded. "Really."

"Well, then it won't hurt if I carry those groceries inside." He moved to pick up the brown paper bags, but Elenore stopped him. Her gaze flashed to the driveway before settling on Evan once again. "Why are you doing this?"

"Doing what? Offering to carry your bags inside?"

"You can't stay here, Detective. If Daddy comes home and finds you here, he'll be angry."

Evan straightened. "Angry with you, you mean?"

She averted her gaze. "Yes."

"Elenore," he began, only to release a sigh and step away from her.

She watched him go, relief and longing warring inside her. She wanted to run after him, beg him to take her with him. But Elijah would find her…find them both.

Chapter Nine

Evan drove away from the Griffin place, his heart in his throat. He'd been a detective long enough to understand when someone lived in fear. And Elenore Griffin definitely feared her father.

There had to be something Evan could do to help her out of her situation. But what? His hands were tied without her cooperation. And he doubted she would cooperate.

The look on her face when she'd opened those shoes would forever haunt him. She looked so young and fragile. But she wasn't young, he reminded himself. She was a grown woman. A very beautiful woman.

Was he attracted to Elenore? Of course he wasn't. He felt sorry for her. That was all. She needed his help to get her out of the nightmare she lived in at home. She also needed psychiatric care. Anyone would, after surviving what Elenore had survived.

It was just before noon when Evan arrived at the courthouse in Wexler. He parked in front of the building and entered through the double doors.

The deputy posted at the metal detector sent Evan a nod and waved him through. "Detective."

Evan returned his greeting and strode to the judge's chamber at the end of the hall. He rapped on the door.

"Enter," Judge Powell barked, impatience evident in his tone.

Opening the door, Evan stepped inside. "Judge Powell. We haven't been formally introduced. I'm—"

"Detective Ramirez," the judge finished for him. "I know who you are. What can I do for you, Detective?"

Evan closed the door. "I was hoping you could answer some questions for me."

The judge waved a hand toward one of the leather chairs in front of his desk. "What sort of questions?"

After Evan was seated, he rested his booted foot on his bent knee and faced the judge with a critical eye. "Does the name Elenore Griffin mean anything to you?"

He didn't flinch. "Should it?"

"You tell me. You oversaw her father's trial about twelve years ago. Elenore would have been eight years old then."

Judge Powell leaned back in his seat, his fingers locked together over his protruding gut. "You expect me to remember a trial that far back? Who was her father?"

"Elijah Griffin."

"Now that name, I recognize. He's been in my courtroom a time or two. What about him?"

If Evan hadn't made it his life's work to look for those small, telltale signs of emotions that most people missed, he might not have ever noticed the slight flicker in the judge's eyes when he'd first mentioned Elenore Griffin's name.

Yeah, Judge Powell was definitely hiding something. "Tell me, Judge, why did you let Elijah Griffin walk? And why give him back custody of his daughter? The same daughter he'd beaten and molested all her young life?"

The judge leaned forward, his eyes narrowing in anger. "Now you listen to me, you young punk of a detective. I realize you're new in this town and obviously trying to make a name for yourself, but you won't do that by harassing me. You're barking up the wrong tree, boy. I suggest you cool your heels before I have them shoved up your arrogant little behind."

"Are you threatening me?" Evan bit out between clenched teeth.

The judge rose to his full height and straightened his robe. "I don't need to threaten you, son. I own this town. The quicker you realize that, the better off you'll be. Now, if you'll excuse me, I have court to oversee." And with that, he strode from the room without a backward glance.

Evan left as well, his mind reeling from the conversation he'd just had with the judge. He'd definitely struck a nerve with the man.

Did Elijah Griffin have something on Judge Powell? And if so…what?

Pulling out his cell phone, Evan put in a call to the sheriff.

"Sheriff King," Donnie announced, answering on the second ring.

"Hey, it's Ramirez." Evan waited until he passed the deputy at the metal detector before continuing. "Are you at the station?"

"For now. I was about to head over to Gerald's Diner and get me a burger. I haven't eaten all day, and I'm about to go down on one knee."

Evan would have laughed if he wasn't still boiling from his talk with the judge. "Mind if I join you?"

"Sure thing, Detective. I'll see you there." He ended the call.

Unlocking his car, Evan slid behind the wheel and put the key in the ignition. He sat there for long moments, staring at the doors to that courthouse, then a thought occurred to him. *Powell's wife.* He would go speak with the man's wife.

Evan had noticed a wedding band on the judge's finger right off the bat. If Powell had been married for more than twelve years, perhaps his wife would remember Elijah Griffin. And maybe…just maybe, she would remember his trial.

* * * *

"You did what?" Donnie set his glass of tea down on the table and stared at Evan as if he'd sprouted wings.

"He knows something, Sheriff. I could see it in his eyes."

Donnie threw an arm out to his side before clearing his throat and lowering his voice. "Be that as it may, you can't just waltz into the judge's office halfcocked and accuse him of throwing a trial."

"I wasn't halfcocked," Evan shot back. "And you should have seen the look he gave me when I mentioned Elenore Griffin's name."

The sheriff ran a hand down his face. "What did he say about her?"

"He denied knowing her. Claimed he didn't recall anyone by that name."

Donnie's cheeks turned a deep shade of red. "That lying piece of garbage," he hissed, glancing around as if worried he'd been overheard.

He met Evan's gaze once more. "He remembers her, all right. The entire town remembers her. It was big news around here for a long time. Why would he lie about that?"

Evan shrugged. "My guess is that Elijah Griffin has something on him. Something big enough that Powell has protected the low-life all these years to keep him quiet."

"I've often wondered about that myself," Donnie admitted.

Evan studied the sheriff's somber expression. "Do you know Powell's wife?"

"Which one? He's had at least three that I know of."

That was interesting news, Evan thought. "The one he was married to when Elijah went to trial."

Donnie seemed to consider that for a moment. "I believe that was Felicia Caswell. Last I heard, she moved to Montgomery not long after her divorce from Powell."

"Can you get me an address?"

"Jesus, Evan. If you're wrong about Powell, and he gets wind that you're questioning his ex…"

"He won't. Besides, I don't believe I'm wrong about him."

Chapter Ten

"Elle?"

Elenore jumped at the sound of her father's voice. She hadn't heard him come home.

She hurried from her bedroom and met him in the kitchen. "Dinner is almost done, Daddy."

"It smells good, too," he praised her, catching her off guard.

He opened his mouth to say something else, but then his gaze dropped to her new shoes.

His demeanor changed instantly. "Where did those come from?"

Evan's words resounded through her mind. "I found them at the thrift shop in town. They were only three dollars. And my other pair of shoes finally gave out. One of them ripped open on the side." Which wasn't a lie.

He continued to study her. "Did you buy them out of the grocery money?"

"I'm sorry, Daddy. I'll take them back. I—"

"Forget it." He waved her apology aside. "You can keep the shoes."

Afraid to believe that he meant it, she nervously twisted her hands in front of her and waited for him to change his mind.

She breathed a sigh of relief when he absently stepped around her and disappeared into his room.

What was going on with him? He hadn't been drinking, that much she could tell. No, something else was on his mind besides her, for once.

She hurried over to the stove, lifted the lid on the pot of stew, and then pulled the biscuits from the oven.

Her father would be in an even better mood when he tasted the dinner she'd made.

Elenore had spent the afternoon cleaning the house and preparing the evening meal.

She told herself the new shoes were responsible for the tiny spark of happiness she'd felt throughout the day, but she wasn't so sure. It couldn't have been because of the detective. *No, not him.*

Evan had been the first man besides Clarence, the mailman, to actually give Elenore a gift without wanting something from her in return. She wasn't sure what to make of it. Regardless of Evan's recent show of generosity, the detective was still a man. And all men were evil. Weren't they?

Elijah came out of his room, holding a suitcase in his hands. "I have to leave for a while."

Elenore's mouth dropped open. "W-where are you going?" She hated how she stuttered when in his presence.

"The law is asking questions about me in town. I need to disappear for a few days until this all dies down."

She wanted to ask why the police were asking questions about him, but she held her tongue. It would only anger him.

"I need you to do something for me. Are you listening, girl?"

Elenore nodded, her fingers fidgeting in front of her.

"Screw the detective."

Her heart flipped over in her chest. "Daddy, I—"

He dropped his suitcase and grabbed her around the throat. "You do what I tell you, or so help me God, you'll live to regret it."

Terror was instant.

His fingers tightened around her throat. "Once you've finished with him, you take your butt into town and tell the sheriff that he forced you."

No! her mind screamed as she stared into her father's manic eyes. He wanted her to accuse Evan of hurting her. She couldn't do it.

"If he ain't behind bars by the time I get back, you better start digging a hole. Because that's exactly where you'll find yourself. Six feet under."

He shoved her away from him hard enough her hip hit the corner of the table.

She bit back a cry of pain and scrambled farther away. An oily film of desperation settled over her. Her father had just threatened to kill her. And she had no doubt that he meant it.

He turned away and strode over to the mantle above the old brick fireplace in the living room.

Flipping the lid open on a cigar box that rested on top, he removed a wad of cash.

Elenore knew he kept a certain amount of money in there, but she didn't dare touch it.

Stuffing the cash into the pocket of his jeans, he stormed past her, plucked up his suitcase, and hurried toward the front door.

He stopped with his hand on the knob and looked at her over his shoulder. "You remember what I said."

Jerking the door open, he left without another word.

Elenore waited until she heard his truck leave the drive before she dropped heavily into a chair at the kitchen table and allowed the tears she'd been holding back to finally fall…

Chapter Eleven

Evan pulled up along the curb in front of Felicia Caswell's nice brick home in Montgomery, Alabama.

The yard appeared freshly mowed, and the shrubs surrounding the house neatly trimmed.

A white sedan was parked in the drive, with a license plate registered to Miss Caswell.

Evan climbed from his car, trailed up to the front door, and rang the bell.

A middle-aged woman opened the door, her dark hair cut short and framing her face. Leeriness shone from her eyes. "May I help you?"

"Miss Caswell?" Evan asked, holding her gaze.

"Yes. What can I do for you?"

Evan removed his wallet from his pocket and showed her his badge. "I'm a detective with the Haverty County Sheriff's Department, here on unofficial business. I was wondering if you wouldn't mind answering a few questions about your ex-husband, Judge Powell."

She moved to close the door in his face.

"It's about a young woman back in Wexler," Evan rushed out. "Her name is Elenore Griffin."

The door slowly opened wider. "What about her?"

"Please, Miss Caswell. If I may?" He gestured toward the opening in the door.

She hesitated a moment and then stepped back. "Come in."

"Thank you, ma'am." He stepped inside.

Miss Caswell's home was as neat on the inside as it was on the out. It smelled of vanilla, which gave it a warm, inviting feel.

"Have a seat, Detective." She waved toward a sofa that rested beneath two windows along the wall.

Evan sat and waited for her to lower herself into an oversized floral chair across from him.

She crossed her legs, her hands folded in her lap. "I have somewhere to be in half an hour, so I'd appreciate it if we could make this quick."

Evan nodded and sat forward on the edge of the couch. "How long were you married to Judge Powell?"

"Martin and I were together a total of four years. What is this about, Detective?"

"Are you familiar with a man named Elijah Griffin?"

Something flickered in her gaze. "I don't know him personally, but I'm aware of who he is. Why do you ask?"

Might as well rip the Band-Aid off quickly, Evan thought before blurting out, "Was there ever any indication that your husband and Elijah Griffin had personal dealings outside of the courts?"

Felica's expression turned passive, but the leeriness remained in her eyes. "Not that I'm aware of. Is there a point here?"

Evan wasn't so sure she was telling the truth, so he pushed. "Are you certain? Please, this is extremely important."

"I am telling the truth." She shifted in her chair, a sign of her uncomfortableness.

"He can't hurt you, Miss Caswell. Powell will never know I was here. You have my word."

Indecision flashed across her face.

Evan sat forward a little more. "There are three people missing from Wexler. People who were associated with Elijah Griffin. I believe he had something to do with the disappearances. I also believe he's holding something over

Powell's head, something big enough to ensure he's untouchable. Now, think harder, Miss Caswell. Did Powell ever mention anything to you about Elijah Griffin?"

Her fingers began to knead the material of her pants. "Were…" she began, only to clear her throat and start anew. "The missing people… Are they young girls?"

That gave Evan pause. "No. Actually they're men. Why would you ask if they were young girls?"

Tears sparkled in Felicia's eyes, but she blinked them back. "When Martin and I divorced, he paid me a large sum of money to keep his personal business out of the courts. We kept the divorce quiet for the most part. I walked away with the money, and he got to keep his secrets."

"Secrets?" Evan pressed.

She continued in a low, unsteady voice. "I loved Martin. He showered me with gifts, a fine home, and vacations to places I had never been before."

Evan remained quiet, understanding that he needed to allow her time to work up the courage to speak about her past with Powell.

"We had the perfect marriage," she whispered, more to herself than to Evan. "Until I found him online one night, watching a video of a man abusing a young girl."

Evan stilled. "Young girl?"

"Yes." She nodded, her gaze becoming unfocused, as if recalling the incident. "He claimed it was part of a case he was trying and demanded I forget what I saw."

"Did you recognize the girl in the video?"

She shook her head. "Not at that time. I tried to block it out, and I was able to for a while. I wanted to believe him, Detective. I wanted to with all my heart. But suspicion and doubt began to fester. Something changed in our marriage after that. The suspicions I experienced after seeing that video plagued me daily. Intimacy became strained to say the least. Then one day while Martin was at work, I opened his laptop."

Evan's heartbeat kicked up a notch. "What did you find in the laptop, Miss Caswell?"

The tears she'd obviously been trying to fight spilled down her cheeks. "More horrific videos with that same girl. They—they were horrendous. Her name was listed at the top of the web page."

"Her name?" Evan prompted in a low, soothing voice. He needed her to keep talking.

She nodded, her gaze still glassy with tears. "I recognized it from the trial she was involved in."

"What was the girl's name, Miss Caswell?"

Her tears fell in earnest. "Elenore Griffin."

Evan stood, grabbed some tissue from an end table, and handed them to the now sobbing woman. "I know this is difficult for you, but I need you to keep going, if you can."

She wiped at her eyes and nose with the tissue. "There were prices listed beneath the video. Large sums of money, as if she were being auctioned." Her voice broke. "Sold to the highest bidder."

Rage filled Evan at the woman's words, but he kept his voice calm and passive. Barely. "Tell me everything you saw, Miss Caswell."

She continued to cry. "I should have said something. I'm just as guilty as Martin. I should have gone to the authorities. But I was too afraid. I didn't know who all Martin had in his pocket, and I didn't have proof that he'd done anything wrong."

Meeting Evan's gaze once more, she sobbed. "Martin told me the video was part of a case he'd been trying. But I checked his case log. There was nothing in writing anywhere to do with that girl, other than the custody case with her father."

"Did you confront Powell about the new videos you'd found?" Evan asked, still managing to remain calm in the face of what had unfolded.

She shook her head. "No, but I started digging deeper, checking the internet history, listening in on his phone calls."

"And did you find anything else?"

"Yes," she answered in a wooden voice. "Martin received several phone calls from a woman. I heard her mention the Griffin girl's name more than once."

Evan nodded for her to continue. "What did she say about Elenore?"

"They spoke in code for the most part. But I heard Martin ask her if the price was still the same. When the woman said yes, he hung up."

Evan's mind was now blown. "Did Powell ever say the woman's name?"

Miss Caswell shook her head. "No, but during one of the brief phone calls, he'd gotten angry with her and said, *'You're a prostitute. Don't ever forget who you're dealing with.'* The woman grew angry in return and threatened Martin with the Griffin girl's father."

"You didn't happen to make copies of those videos, did you?"

"No," the woman confirmed, sending disappointment crashing into Evan. "But I told Martin that I wanted a divorce shortly after that."

Evan rubbed at his forehead. "What happened then?"

"He tried to convince me to stay, but I couldn't. I just wanted out of his life and out of that county. I wanted to forget everything I'd seen and heard in that house. When he refused to give me a divorce, I threatened him. Told him I would expose him for a pedophile. He informed me that it would be my word against his. But in the end, he paid me a large sum of money and gave me the divorce I wanted so desperately. I left and never looked back."

Evan rested his hands together between his knees. "If I can gather enough evidence to indict him, would you be willing to testify to what you witnessed?"

"No." She got to her feet. "I will not. I've told you everything I know. I'll not be involved beyond that. Now, if you'll excuse me, I'm running late for an appointment."

And just like that, she dismissed him.

Evan drove away from Miss Caswell's brick home, his mind reeling from everything he'd learned. Elijah Griffin had sold Elenore to the highest bidder, when she'd been eight years old. Sold her to men like the judge, to do with as they pleased.

Nausea rolled through Evan. Elenore Griffin had never stood a chance. No wonder she remained in her abusive situation. It was all she knew.

Evan replayed Miss Caswell's words over and over in his mind. Yet he kept coming back to the unknown woman, Powell had spoken with on that phone. *"You're a prostitute. Don't ever forget who you're dealing with."*

So, Elijah didn't deal with Powell on a personal level. He'd used a prostitute as a middleman. But who? It wasn't as if Wexler's streets were crawling with hookers. Evan was sure there were some in Haverty County who sold their bodies for money. Some, but not many.

If he were still in Atlanta, searching for a particular prostitute wouldn't be an easy feat. But thankfully, he wasn't in Atlanta any longer. Wexler would be a heck of a lot easier to locate a hooker in. He hoped.

Chapter Twelve

Elenore walked the two-mile trek into town, her emotions pushed to the far recesses of her mind. Elijah had ordered her to seduce the detective—something that sickened Elenore, even more than her visits from the sadistic, Bill.

A shudder passed through her at the memory of Bill's last visit. He'd been sodomizing her for as long as she could remember. Most of the men her father sold her to did. But Bill was especially cruel in his preferences. The more painful it was for her—the more she screamed—the more he enjoyed it.

Elenore hated them all…but not as much as she loathed Bill.

The small town of Wexler lay just ahead. She pushed her thoughts to the back of her mind and walked the short distance to the sheriff's office.

She passed Gerald's Diner on her way, her stomach growling from the delicious aroma the place exuded.

Keeping her head down, she hurried on past, hoping no one inside recognized her.

No such luck.

The bell over the door chimed, and a feminine voice called out. "Elenore?"

Pretending she didn't hear her, Elenore picked up her pace.

"Elenore, wait!"

With no other choice, Elenore slowly turned to find Lucy Jackson, a girl she'd gone to school with, currently hurrying in her direction.

Lucy stopped a couple of feet in front of her. "I haven't seen you in forever, Elenore. How have you been?"

Elenore couldn't hold her gaze, so great was her shame.

Where Lucy had excelled in school, Elenore had dropped out in the tenth grade. She'd had no choice. The school had asked too many questions about her bruises and injuries.

Where Lucy had been well liked, Elenore had been bullied. But not by Lucy. No, Lucy Jackson had probably been one of the only students in the Wexler public school system who'd treated Elenore with kindness, didn't make fun of her clothes, and sat with her during lunch when no one else would.

"Elenore?"

It took Elenore a moment to respond. She quickly glanced up, her arms unconsciously folding over her chest. "I'm okay."

An awkward silence fell between them. Then Lucy reached up and touched Elenore on the arm. "Wow, that looks painful. How'd you get that?"

Elenore realized Lucy referred to a large bruise on her upper arm. She covered it with her hand. "The cow kicked me when I was milking her."

"Ouch," Lucy answered, motioning toward the diner. "I was just about to have lunch. Would you like to join me?"

Man, would she ever. Elenore wanted to say yes so badly her stomach growled in agreement. But instead, she murmured, "I can't. I'm in a hurry. Maybe next time."

Lucy looked disappointed, but she merely nodded. "Okay. Well, it was good seeing you again. Take care."

"You too," Elenore whispered, spinning on her heel and walking away.

She hurried down the sidewalk toward the sheriff's office, her gaze flicking to the courthouse across the road, the place sworn to protect the innocent...the children. But it hadn't protected her. She'd been sent back into a Hell of her father's making. A Hell she would never escape from.

Elenore had no family, no education or money. She wouldn't get far, even if she tried. And she'd tried once, long ago. But Elijah had hunted her down and dragged her back. She'd suffered a broken wrist and collarbone for her insolence. Elijah had raped her in the vilest of ways, including using objects he'd found in the kitchen.

She had been forced to stay in her room for days with nothing to eat and only water from the bathroom to drink, while her broken bones were left unattended. Elenore had never known as much pain as she had in that week. She'd never attempted to leave again.

Stepping inside the sheriff's office, she awkwardly approached a man sitting behind a window. "Is Detective Ramirez here?"

The man looked up over the top of his glasses. "He's in his office. Is there something I can help you with?"

Elenore shook her head. "No. I need to speak with the detective."

"Okay, Miss. I'll see if he's busy. One minute."

The man disappeared for long moments only to return with the Ramirez in tow.

"Elenore?" Evan stepped through a doorway, his eyebrows raised in question. "What are you doing here?"

Her stomach knotted up. How was she supposed to go through with it? She had no idea how to seduce a man. And even if she did, she didn't want to. The thought sickened her. "I… It's nothing."

She spun on her heel and fled.

Evan caught up with her on the sidewalk. "Wait."

Elenore continued forward, fear mingling with regret. She would suffer greatly at the hands of Elijah when he returned, but she couldn't seduce the detective.

Evan suddenly grabbed her by the hand. "Hey?"

With no choice but to stop or drag him along with her, Elenore halted her steps.

She kept her head down. "I...I was just looking for a ride home. But it's not that far. I can walk."

"Nonsense." He gently squeezed her hand. "I can give you a lift. It'll give us an opportunity to talk."

He dug his keys from his pocket and unlocked the door to his car parked along the curb.

Elenore allowed him to help her into the passenger side and then watched him round the vehicle and get in behind the wheel.

The air conditioner came on when he started the engine. "You should have called me. I would have given you a lift into town. Especially at this hour. It would've been dark by the time you made it home."

"I don't have a phone."

He remained quiet while he pulled away from the curb and then asked, "How did you get that bruise on your arm? It's not the same one as before."

Elenore wanted to crawl into a hole. "The cow kicked me when I was milking her."

Evan sent her a side-eye look that told her he wasn't buying her explanation. "Did Elijah do that?"

Looking down at the bruise in question, Elenore shook her head. "No. I told you, the—"

"The cow did it. I heard you."

An uncomfortable silence settled between them while Elenore's mind scrambled for something to say.

Evan beat her to it. "Have you ever heard your father mention anything about Judge Powell?"

Elenore shook her head. "Not that I can remember."

"Are you sure?" he pressed, turning onto the clay road that led to her house.

"I'm sure."

A few minutes later, Evan pulled into Elenore's drive. He switched off the car, came around to her side, and opened her door.

Elenore had never had a man open a car door for her. Of course, she'd never been in a car with a man other than Elijah.

Evan glanced at the house. "Your father isn't home?"

Now's your chance, Elenore. Do it. "He's out of town."

With a nod, Evan turned to go.

"I made a pot of stew," Elenore blurted. "Would you like some?"

Evan continued around the car. "I really should go. I have to finish up some paperwork back at the station."

"Please?" she whispered, her heart pounding in a painful rhythm. It was now or never.

He stopped on the other side of the car and opened his door.

She could see the indecision in his eyes.

"I don't want to eat alone, Detective."

After staring at her for long moments, Evan closed his car door. "Stew sounds good."

Chapter Thirteen

Evan followed Elenore toward the house against his better judgement.

Everything inside him screamed to turn around and leave, but his feet continued to move forward.

He wasn't sure if his decision to accept her invitation to eat stemmed from pity or attraction. Because, honestly, he felt both for her.

She opened the back door and disappeared into the kitchen.

And like a fool, Evan entered behind her.

He found her standing at the stove.

She shyly glanced at him before turning on the fire beneath a pot, picking up a ladle, and stirring the contents. "Have a seat, Detective."

God, but she was beautiful. Evan moved to the small kitchen table and lowered himself into a chair. He was playing with fire by being alone with her, and he knew it.

He studied her small shoulders. Though the dress she wore was a size too big, it tapered in at her waist, hugging her rounded hips.

Evan shook off his inappropriate thoughts and moved to join her at the stove, needing something—anything to do but stare at her shapely figure. "What's in the stew?"

She flinched as if he'd startled her somehow. "Beef, potatoes, tomatoes, and a few other vegetables from the garden."

"It smells wonderful," he softly admitted, staring at her profile.

She cleared her throat, a nervous energy surrounding her. "Excuse me."

Evan backed up to allow her room to step around him.

She disappeared around the corner, returning a moment later with a bottle of whiskey.

Taking down two glasses, she poured a generous amount into each and then handed him one.

Surprised, Evan shook his head. "I can't. I have to drive home."

Elenore downed her whiskey, her face scrunching up immediately afterward. "The food will soak up the alcohol."

Evan knew he should decline, march out that door and not look back. Instead, he accepted the glass and brought it to his lips. A small drink wouldn't hurt anything.

She sent him a soft smile.

If Evan had thought her beautiful before, she was downright gorgeous when she smiled. "You should do that more often."

"Do what?"

"Smile."

"Oh." She trailed back to the stove to dip them up two bowls of stew.

Evan waited until she set the bowls on the table along with the biscuits before taking a seat.

She joined him, gifting him with another timid smile.

He picked up his spoon and took a bite of the food. It had to be the best stew he'd ever tasted. "This is delicious."

"Thank you, Detective."

"Please, call me Evan." He'd just dissolved his professional relationship with Elenore. Actually, he silently admonished, that ship had sailed the moment he'd agreed to join her for dinner.

Once the meal was finished, Elenore gathered their dishes and carried them to the sink.

Evan joined her, offering to dry what she washed.

His hand brushed against hers, and both of them stilled.

Leave, he repeated over and over in his mind. Yet his body continued to stand there.

Elenore awkwardly moved away. But to his surprise, she poured them both another whiskey.

Warning bells were going off with a vengeance by this point. Still, Evan didn't leave. Like an idiot, he accepted the drink. He downed it in one fell swoop, loving the feel of the burn on its way down.

She took the glass from him, her body pressing against his as she leaned around him to set it on the counter behind him.

Evan thought his heart would burst through his chest, so great was his lust. "What are you doing?"

Elenore didn't answer. She simply backed up a step, her fingers going to the button at the top of her dress.

"Elenore?" Evan reached up to stop her, his mind protesting her actions, even as his body prayed she wouldn't stop.

"I want you," she whispered, her fingers continuing their movements.

The dress slipped off her shoulders to pool around her waist.

Evan's gaze dropped to her bra-covered breasts. "We can't..."

She reached behind her and unhooked the bra before he finished his protest.

"Elenore... I..." He had no words to describe how sexy she was in that moment.

She reached up and laid her hand against his stomach.

Evan was lost.

His eyes slid shut with the feel of her hand on him. His breathing quickly grew uneven, and an urgency to possess her overtook him.

He told himself he did nothing wrong. They were both consenting adults and— *"Until I found him online one night, watching a video of a man abusing a young girl."* Felicia Caswell's words slid through Evan's mind like oil to drown out the rest of his thoughts.

Evan jerked back as if burned. He stared down into Elenore's confused eyes, purposely avoiding looking at her breasts. "I'm sorry. I can't do this."

Elenore visibly swallowed. "You don't want me?"

Was that fear he detected in her voice? "Want you? I want you so bad, I ache. But it's not right. Not like this."

Moving toward the back door, Evan noticed his hand shook as he twisted the knob. "Thank you for dinner, Elenore. It was delicious."

He practically ran from the place.

Once inside his vehicle, he blew out an unsteady breath, started the engine, and put the car in reverse. His entire body was alive with need. A need he couldn't afford to give in to.

What on earth had he been thinking? He'd almost had sex with Elenore Griffin.

Chapter Fourteen

Elenore stood rooted to the spot, long after the detective's rapid departure. She had failed to seduce him.

How was she going to explain to her father that she hadn't been able to tempt the detective? Elijah would hurt her. Of that, she could be sure.

She stepped out of her dress and trailed to her bedroom to slip on her tattered gown. Numbness from the whiskey mingled with her anxiety. Elijah would never understand that she couldn't tempt the detective out of his clothes.

Part of Elenore was relieved that Evan had turned her down. That meant she didn't have to accuse him of forcing her. Of all the men she wanted to hurt, Evan was not one of them.

The sound of the back-door opening caught her off guard. Had the detective changed his mind?

Turning toward her bedroom door, she waited for him to come around the corner.

But it wasn't Evan she saw standing in her doorway.

Bill stepped into her room, holding the dreaded briefcase in his hand.

He placed it on the floor. "What was Detective Ramirez doing here?"

Elenore stumbled back a step, terror instantly filling her.

"Cat got your tongue?" Bill taunted, removing his tie. "I asked you what the detective was doing here."

When she didn't answer, his dark brown eyes narrowed in anger. "Take off the gown and get on the bed."

"Please don't do this," she begged, nearly tripping on the small rug on her floor.

He continued removing his clothes. "It'll be a lot worse for you if I have to tell you again."

Tears of desperation filled her eyes. She gripped the hem of her gown and pulled it over her head, all the while praying for Evan's return.

Bill walked forward, shoving her onto the bed.

She stared up at him in horror, watching while he retrieved the ropes from his case.

"Spread 'em. I want you face up this time."

Elenore knew there would be no use in fighting him. He would only hurt her worse.

She did as he demanded, opening her legs and spreading her arms wide.

The ropes bit into her wrists and ankles as he roughly secured them to the bedposts.

Elenore stared up at the ceiling, allowing her mind to close in on itself, to take her to a place where no one could hurt her. Not even Bill.

Her vision became tunneled, and the room grew dim around her.

Somewhere in the far recesses of her mind, she knew Bill touched her, but the sickening emotions that would normally provoke were dulled to the point where she barely felt them.

His face appeared in her line of sight, hovering above her.

She shut it out, her gaze locking on a place beyond his shoulder.

The pain of his entry nearly pulled her back from the abyss, but she held strong. She wouldn't give him the pleasure of hearing her cry out. She never would again.

* * * *

Elenore spent the next two days, unable to get out of bed. Her entire body ached, and she was pretty certain she had some broken ribs.

Strange that she didn't recall Bill removing her bonds.

He had done things to her, things that most folks wouldn't dream up in their wildest nightmares. But Bill was sadistic. He always had been.

Tears of pain and humiliation spilled from Elenore's eyes. Her safe place hadn't protected her. He'd hurt her bad enough, her mask of numbness had slipped.

The man known only as Bill had been visiting Elenore for as long as she could remember.

She recalled the first time he'd come to the house and entered her room. Elijah had prepared her for him.

Bill hadn't hurt her as much back then. But as time moved on, his visits became more frequent and more twisted.

Elenore had begged her father not to allow Bill back into her room, but Elijah would only beat her and demand she keep his customers happy.

There were others who visited Elenore's room over the years, but none as monstrous as Bill. And out of the others, some even preferred pain and sodomy, but Bill was the only one who ripped into her with objects meant to leave scars.

The viler and more heinous the act, the more Bill enjoyed it. And Elenore prayed nightly that he rotted in the deepest, fieriest pit of Hell imaginable. Truth be told, she prayed they all did.

A knock on the kitchen door brought her swollen eyes open a crack. She knew it wouldn't be Bill. He never knocked.

She held perfectly still, hoping that whoever stood on the back porch would give up and go away. She couldn't allow anyone to see what had been done to her.

The sound of the door opening shattered her hope.

"Elenore?"

The detective's voice sent panic slicing through her. There was nothing she could do but lie there, her heart slamming against her ribs.

He stepped around the corner. "Elen— Oh my God!"

Evan rushed across the room, his face a mask of sorrow and rage. "Jesus, baby!"

Elenore moaned in pain as his arms slipped beneath her nude form.

He lifted her, holding her high against his chest.

Snatching up a blanket, he quickly covered her nakedness, all the while repeating the word, *Jesus*.

Elenore wasn't sure if he even realized what he said.

"I'm going to get you some help," he choked out, running through the house toward the kitchen.

He opened the back door, turning sideways in order to pass through with her in his arms. "Ah, God, Elenore. Who did this to you?"

Elenore didn't speak. She couldn't if she'd wanted to. It hurt to part her lips, let alone gather the strength to form words.

Evan ran across the yard, hoisting her up higher in his arms.

With every step he took, more agony sliced through Elenore's body.

He opened the back door to his car and laid her gently on the seat. Seconds passed like hours.

And then he was backing out of the drive, speaking on his cell phone as he went. "This is

Detective Ramirez with the Haverty County Sheriff's Office. I'm en route to you with a twenty-year-old female who presents with multiple lacerations and evidence of strangulation. We'll be there in five minutes."

Elenore listened to him put in another call to Sheriff Donnie King, who apparently wasn't in. "Sheriff, it's Evan. I need you to meet me at Wexler General. I'm bringing in Elenore Griffin. She's been hurt."

He ended the call and tore out onto the dirt road, speaking over his shoulder as he drove. "Elenore, are you still with me?"

She couldn't answer. The last thought she had before darkness overtook her once more was of how angry Elijah would be when he returned home to find her gone.

Chapter Fifteen

Evan slowed his car to a crawl on the washboard dirt road leading back to town. Taking the ruts in the road at a high rate of speed was causing Elenore too much pain.

Someone had raped her. Of that, he had no doubt. The blood on the insides of her thighs was a testament to that fact.

Her eyes were blue and swollen shut. She had a cut next to her bottom lip and lacerations on her wrists and ankles.

Rage unlike any he'd experienced before overtook him in that moment. How long had she been lying there, unable to call for help? Not that it would have done any good. She'd already told him she didn't have a phone.

Guilt assailed him next. He shouldn't have left her there. He should have demanded she let him take her to the shelter in town. She was in a bad situation at that farm. Evan had known it from the first time he'd heard the stories about her in town.

"You're safe now, Elenore. I'm going to get you some help."

Her answer was a soft keening sound that tore at his already shattered heart.

The dirt road finally came to an end. Evan punched the gas and drove like a speed demon the rest of the way to the hospital.

A man wearing scrubs waited out front next to a wheelchair obviously meant for Elenore.

Evan threw the car into park, jumped out, and opened the back door.

"I got you, sweetheart." He lifted Elenore's small form into his arms, careful to keep the blanket draped over her. He rushed through the sliding double doors to the emergency room without bothering with the wheelchair.

"Right this way." A nurse waved him over to a bed that sat behind a curtain.

Evan followed close, his entire body strung tight with adrenaline.

He carefully deposited Elenore onto the bed.

"What happened to her?" The nurse lifted one of Elenore's eyelids.

It took Evan a moment to answer. "I don't know. I found her like this."

The nurse nodded, checking Elenore's other eye. "You got a name, sweetheart?"

"Elenore," Evan answered for her. "Elenore Griffin."

Recognition registered in the nurse's eyes. "I'm familiar."

A short, balding man wearing a white coat suddenly appeared. He pulled a small light from the pocket of his coat and went about doing the same checks the nurse had just done. "What do we have here?"

Evan gave the man all the information he could think of while the nurse started an IV in Elenore's arm.

"Do you know if she has any family? I'll need to find out if she's allergic to any medications." The doctor gently opened her mouth to check inside.

"We have her records," the nurse quietly stated. "It's Elenore Griffin."

The doctor paused for a second as if understanding dawned. "Let's get her stabilized and then take her to the back for X-rays."

Evan stumbled to the side as another nurse rushed into the small space, demanding room.

The curtain was abruptly jerked closed, shutting him out.

He could hear them working on Elenore, her moans of pain clawing at his insides.

His teeth locked together in an attempt to hold back the string of curses gathering behind them. Had Elijah done this to her? Evan would kill him, but not before beating him to a bloody pulp.

Sheriff Donnie King rounded the corner, his face pale and drawn. "I got your message. What on earth is going on?"

Evan turned toward the waiting room, motioning for the sheriff to follow him. He stopped near the bathrooms on the left. "Elenore Griffin was attacked. She's been beaten pretty bad…and raped."

Donnie dragged a hand down his face. "Was it her father?"

"I don't know," Evan admitted in a low voice. "She was alone when I found her."

The sheriff blew out a weary breath. "Where did you find her?"

Evan opened his mouth to answer, suddenly realizing how his next words would sound. "In her bedroom."

"In her bedroom," Donnie slowly repeated. "Why were you in her bedroom?"

Fully understanding how it would sound, Evan admitted, "I had dinner with her a couple of days ago at her house. I'd left rather abruptly and was feeling bad about it. So, I went back to apologize. When she didn't answer the door, I let myself inside. That's when I found her."

Donnie briefly closed his eyes. "You shouldn't have done that, Detective."

Anger reared its head. "If I hadn't done it, she very well could have lay there and died."

"That's not what I meant, and you know it. Why would you have dinner with her while investigating her father? That house belongs to him. Does he know about your dinner date?"

Evan ground his teeth. "It wasn't a date. And I didn't stay long." He left out the part about the whiskey and Elenore removing her dress.

The sheriff gripped him on the shoulder. "What's done is done. How bad is she?"

"Bad, Sheriff. Really bad. She needs to get out of there before her father kills her."

Donnie blew out a sigh. "She's been told that very thing a dozen times before. But if she doesn't press charges, our hands are tied. And she's never pressed charges."

"But you didn't see what he did to her," Evan argued, growing angrier by the second.

The sheriff's gaze turned weary. "Do we know for sure it was Elijah that did this to her?"

"No." Evan glanced toward the closed curtain in the other room. "But I'd bet my life that it was him."

Donnie nodded. "I'll put out an APB on Elijah. We can bring him in for questioning, but if she doesn't press charges, he walks."

"Even if she does press charges," Evan murmured, still watching that curtain, "he'll end up going before Judge Powell. And we both know how that'll turn out."

Chapter Sixteen

Elenore slowly came awake to the sound of beeping somewhere to her left.

She attempted to sit up, but an agonizing pain in her sides prevented her from moving.

Confused and more than a little disoriented, she sought out the beeping sound, only to realize that it belonged to an alarm on an IV machine. She was in the hospital.

Memory came flooding back with a vengeance. Bill, the ropes, his fists. He'd beaten her with her father's fireplace poker, and then he had assaulted her with it.

The pain of his torment had brought her out of her safe place. She hadn't been able to mentally hide from him any longer. She'd been forced to lie there, fully lucid, enduring the torture he'd inflicted upon her, again and again. A torture that went on for hours.

Elenore stared up at the ceiling in that hospital, her mind numb, even if her body wasn't. She had survived to suffer another day.

Her pain would never end. She knew that as surely as she knew her father would likely kill her and bury her somewhere on the property. Her remains would never be found.

She didn't care. Not anymore. The thought of dying was a welcome reprieve from the torment that was her life.

"You're awake."

Elenore's gaze traveled to a chair parked next to her bed to find Detective Ramirez sitting there. "Detective. How long have I been here?"

"It's Evan. Please. And you've been here for two days."

Two days. Elenore had been in that hospital for two days. Apparently, her father hadn't returned from his trip, else he would have been up there, raising the roof by now.

Evan pushed to his feet. He appeared haggard, and stubble lined his jaw, telling her he hadn't shaved in a while. "How are you feeling? Can I get you anything?"

Why did the detective care about what happened to her? No one had ever cared before. No one.

She shook her head, her mind remaining numb. "I just want to be left alone."

Hurt registered in his eyes, but it left as quickly as it appeared. "I understand. But I need to ask you a couple of questions first."

"Ask," she responded in a flat tone.

"Did your father do this to you?"

"No. My father is out of town."

The detective didn't look convinced. "Do you know who did this to you?"

Bill's dark brown eyes flashed through her mind. "No. He wore a mask."

Leaning down a little closer, Evan softly implored her. "I can't find the man who did this without your help, Elenore. Please think. Do you remember anything at all that might help us identify him? His size, what he was wearing, his voice, anything?"

Elenore looked him straight in the eyes. "Like I said, Detective. He wore a mask."

Evan straightened, disappointment obvious in his countenance. "I'll come back a bit later, once you've had time to rest."

Elenore waited for him to disappear from sight before pushing the call button lying next to her hip.

A heavy-set nurse appeared a moment later, her gray hair secured in a bun at the back of her head. "What can I get for you, Miss Griffin?"

"My clothes."

"Pardon?" The nurse stepped closer to the bed.

"I need my clothes. I'm going home."

The nurse's eyebrows lifted. "You can't leave, Miss Griffin. You're on antibiotics, and you have some bruised ribs."

None of that mattered to Elenore. Nothing mattered anymore except the fact that her ribs weren't broken. "I'm leaving here, with or without your help."

Pity appeared in the older woman's eyes. "Very well. Do you have someone to drive you home?"

Elenore hadn't thought that far ahead. She shook her head. "I have no one."

"I'll see if I can arrange for an ambulance to take you home. In the meantime, why don't you use that button strapped to your bedrail to relieve some of your pain? That's what it's there for."

"Thank you," Elenore numbly muttered, reaching for the small wand with the button on the end. She pressed it several times with her thumb, knowing full well the medication wouldn't release any faster.

Some of her pain finally ebbed.

Minutes ticked by, with Elenore waiting for what seemed an eternity for the nurse to return with a nonemergency transport ride home.

But it wasn't the nurse's face she saw in her now, sleepy vision. "Detective?" she slurred, blinking to stay awake. "I told you, I don't know anything."

Evan ran a hand through his disheveled hair. "I didn't come here to drill you, Elenore. I came to offer my help."

Elenore blinked with heavy eyelids. "Your help?"

He nodded. "I know your history with your father. I read the reports. I also know that you're afraid of him…and rightfully so."

She opened her mouth to argue, but he held up a hand to stop her. "Just hear me out."

When she remained quiet, he continued. "There's a hospital in Montgomery, equipped with some of the finest doctors in the south. Doctors who can help you to cope with everything you've been through. You'd have around-the-clock care, and no one would know you're there but the sheriff and me."

Elenore strained to follow along, his words seeming to fade in and out. "But my father—"

"Would never find you. And even if he did, he couldn't reach you in there. I can have a guard posted outside your door, with orders not to allow anyone inside your room without your permission."

Elenore seemed to momentarily lose focus. Flashes of her father's face blended with images of Bill, Judge Powell, and a few more men she could barely recall scattered throughout her mind.

She attempted to follow Evan's words. "I can't go to a place like that. I have no money to pay with."

Evan reached up and tucked some of her hair behind her ear. "Don't think about that right now. Besides, the state will help if you're indigent."

"Indigent?"

He glanced down at his hands. "In poverty. Without a means to pay."

"You mean poor," she whispered, her voice seeming to come from far away.

For some reason, his fingers gently touching her hair didn't sicken Elenore.

"Yes, Elenore…poor," she heard him softly confess before she gave up the fight and welcomed the darkness.

Chapter Seventeen

Flagstaff Mental Hospital. Montgomery, Alabama

Two Weeks Later

Evan stood outside the door to Doctor Ingram's office, debating on whether to knock. He hadn't seen Elenore since her arrival at Flagstaff Mental hospital six days ago.

It had taken Evan a week to convince Elenore to check herself in. She'd been adamant about going home after her visit to the emergency room, claiming that her father would be irate when he came home to find her gone. She'd also argued that no one would be there to feed the animals.

Evan had assured her that he would swing by the house to make sure the animals were fed, at least until her father returned. *If* he returned.

The door abruptly opened, and Doctor Ingram stood there with a surprised look on his face. "Detective Ramirez. You startled me."

"Likewise," Evan admitted, unsure of what to do next.

Ingram extended his hand, which Evan immediately accepted.

"May I help you with something, Detective?"

Evan cleared his throat. "I was hoping to talk to you about Elenore. I just went to see her, but the nurse said she's been sedated?"

"Would you care to come in?" the doctor asked, searching Evan's gaze.

"Yes, thank you." Evan waited for the doctor to take a step back before he entered the room and stood in front of the man's desk.

"Please," Ingram murmured, flicking a wrist in the direction of a brown leather chair.

Evan took a seat and waited for Ingram to do the same. "Elijah hasn't attempted to see his daughter, has he?"

Ingram shook his head. "There have been no visitors other than yourself, Detective."

Evan let that digest. "How is she doing? Are you making any headway with her?"

Ingram pushed his glasses up on his nose. "You do understand that I cannot discuss Miss Griffin's case with you?"

"I know," Evan replied, shifting to a more comfortable position in his seat. "I just want to be sure she's getting the best care. She's been through an awful lot in her young life."

The doctor nodded. "It's a shame what's been done to her, done to so many of my patients. We can't erase their pasts; we can only try to help them heal enough to have somewhat of a productive future."

"And will she? Elenore, I mean. Will she have a productive future?"

"I certainly hope so, Detective."

Evan rubbed his palms along the front of his jeans. "May I see her?"

Ingram stood. "Of course. But keep in mind that she is heavily medicated and might not remember that you were here."

Evan got to his feet as well. "Why is she medicated?"

"It's necessary for her safety."

The doctor's words caught Evan off guard. "Is she suicidal?"

Ingram held his gaze. "It's hard to say. But considering everything she's been through both mentally and physically, I thought it best to keep her in a relaxed state for the time being."

"I understand." Evan followed Doctor Ingram out of his office and down the hall.

Nurses and orderlies were bustling about, busy caring for the mentally ill. It hurt Evan to think of Elenore being among them, medicated and alone. But the hospital was the best place she could be at the moment, and he knew that.

The doctor stopped outside Elenore's room and nodded to the guard posted there.

The guard immediately unlocked the door and pushed it open.

Evan absently thanked him before stepping inside.

Elenore sat in a chair, facing two bar-covered windows. She looked so small sitting there in a pale blue gown.

Her feet were crossed at the ankles beneath her chair. Evan noticed she wore yellow socks with the nonskid material on the bottoms. Her hair hung loose around her shoulders, appearing clean and brushed.

A tray of food rested untouched on a bedside table next to her elbow.

"Elenore?" Evan softly called, moving deeper into the room.

She continued to stare out that window.

Evan grabbed a small wooden chair from against the wall and dragged it over to her side.

"Elenore?" He took a seat, relieved when she slowly turned her head in his direction.

She seemed confused for a moment before recognition registered in her crystal-blue eyes. "Detective?"

Relieved that she wasn't medicated to the point of being zombified, Evan sent her a soft smile. "How are you feeling?"

"Still a little sore, but the doctor says I'm healing."

"That's great news. It's good to see you."

She continued to stare at him to the point where he grew uncomfortable. "How long will I be here?"

Her question surprised him. "Do you want to leave?"

Confusion flickered in her eyes. "I don't know. Has Daddy been here?"

Evan shook his head. "No, he hasn't. He can't get to you here, Elenore."

"How will I pay for this place?" She turned back to her window-gazing.

Evan touched her on the arm, pulling his hand back when she shrank from his touch. "Don't you worry about that, Elenore. The state is picking up the bill. You just relax and get better. Okay?"

She slowly nodded and then met his gaze once again. "Has my daddy been here?"

Evan's stomach tightened with pity. She obviously didn't recall just asking him that same question not a minute before. "No, Elenore. Elijah hasn't been here."

After staying with her a few more minutes, Evan eased to his feet. "I'll come back to visit you as soon as I can."

When she didn't respond, he quietly left the room.

Chapter Eighteen

Evan arrived back in Wexler a little over an hour later to an insane amount of activity.

Sheriff King paced the floor at the station, pale-faced and more than a little agitated. "Where have you been? I've left you a dozen messages."

Evan approached the sheriff. "I was in Montgomery, visiting Elenore Griffin at the hospital. I'm sorry, sir. I forgot to turn my ringer back on. What's wrong?"

"Judge Powell is missing."

"Missing?"

Donnie nodded. "His wife came in this morning to report it. Apparently, she's been out of town visiting her sister for a couple of weeks and came home to find him gone."

Evan rested his hand on his hip. "He's probably slung up with a local prostitute."

The sheriff obviously didn't find any humor in Evan's remark, if his expression were any indication. "According to the neighbors, they haven't seen his car in the drive or any lights come on in over a week."

"He could be the one who attacked Elenore," Evan bit out. "If he is, that would explain his disappearance."

Donnie lowered his voice. "Why would Judge Powell attack Elenore?"

Evan filled the sheriff in on everything he'd learned from his visit with Felicia Caswell, ending with, "That young girl Felicia found on Powell's computer was Elenore Griffin."

The sheriff paled. "That's sickening. Did Caswell say why she didn't come forward with that information?"

"She was afraid. And I can't say that I blame her. Though coming forward would have saved poor Elenore from a living Hell, Felicia feared Powell too much to speak up."

Donnie's eyes narrowed. "And Miss Caswell didn't give you the name of the prostitute she'd heard on the phone with Powell?"

Evan shook his head. "She claims she never learned a name."

"Did you believe her?"

"I did." Evan thought about the look on Felicia's face when she'd recalled her dealings with Powell. "She was telling the truth."

The sheriff pulled out his cell phone and put in a call to Charlie, who was probably sitting in Gerald's Diner, where he could normally be found.

After ordering the deputy to go out to Judge Powell's place and see what he could find, Donnie disconnected the call and faced Evan once more. "Let's bring in Elijah Griffin for questioning. My gut tells me he's at the root of all this. Including Hector Gonzalez's disappearance. He was, after all, the last person seen with him."

Evan followed the sheriff outside. "I bet if we dig deep enough, we'd find a connection between Griffin and the other two missing men in Wexler as well. Also, I looked through the arrest records in Haverty County, going back twelve years. I saw only one arrest for prostitution, and that woman is now deceased."

Donnie moved around to the driver's side of his car. "We don't get too many prostitutes in Wexler, Detective. The community is too tight knit. This isn't like Atlanta. You're in the Bible Belt of Alabama now."

Evan strode to his own vehicle, parked directly behind the sheriff's. "A Bible Belt that allowed an eight-year-old little girl to be abused right under their noses."

Weariness settled in the sheriff's eyes. "I know, Detective. Seems like the more religious the church, the more that evil will darken its doors. See you at the Griffin's place."

* * * *

Evan pulled into Elijah Griffin's drive behind the sheriff. He climbed from his vehicle, his gaze touching on everything around him. "I've been out here, feeding the animals every day for the past week, Sheriff. Elijah hasn't been here at all. You think he skipped town with Powell?"

The sheriff shrugged. "Hard to say."

Retrieving his cell phone, Donnie pressed some buttons and brought the phone to his ear.

Evan listened while he questioned someone about Elijah Griffin.

"Elijah hasn't shown up for work in nearly two weeks," Donnie announced as he hung up the call.

"He's in the wind," Evan bit out, marching toward the back of the house.

Donnie caught up with him in a few short strides. "What do you think you're doing?"

"I'm going in."

The sheriff stepped in front of him at the back door. "No, you're not."

"With all due respect, sir, we—"

"If we go inside without a warrant," the sheriff interrupted, cutting off the rest of Evan's words, "anything we find in there will be inadmissible in a court of law. Not to mention, it's an illegal search. You know that."

Evan did know that. "I'll get written permission from Elenore."

"She's in a psych ward, Detective. Anything written by her won't hold up in court, either.

Use your brain, son. You're too emotionally involved and not thinking straight."

The sheriff was right. He *was* too involved. He'd developed feelings for Elenore—feelings that went beyond sympathy. He needed to get a grip, and quick, before he messed around and screwed up any chance of nailing Elijah Griffin to the wall.

Blowing out a defeated breath, Evan backed up a step. "You're right, of course. I don't know what's gotten into me."

"You're human," the sheriff admitted, his gaze sweeping the surrounding area. "There's nothing wrong with being passionate about your job. In fact, it's a welcome reprieve from what the department has had in the past. But you have to rein it in a touch or risk letting that piece of trash Elijah walk."

Evan nodded. He opened his mouth to thank the man, when another thought occurred to him. "Did William Burnham ever investigate Griffin?"

The sheriff brought his attention back to Evan's face. "Many times. Why?"

"I'm just wondering if he might have found something I've overlooked. I'm going to head out to his place and talk to him."

"Wait," Donnie called out after Evan turned to go. "I'll have Charlie come and feed these animals on his way home in the evenings. I don't want you back over here. Understood?"

Evan's jaw tightened, but he didn't argue. "I understand."

Chapter Nineteen

Evan arrived at William Burnham's address ten minutes later. He didn't see a car in the drive.

Striding toward the door, Evan took in his surroundings. A chicken coop sat next to a garden of what appeared to be cabbage and peas of some kind.

The house itself, though old, looked to be in good shape. It had obviously undergone a facelift recently, boasting white paint and black trim around the windows.

A wooden swing hung from the large porch, with two ferns resting on either side of it.

Burnham had a paradise on the outskirts of town. The perfect place to live out his retirement.

Evan stepped up onto the porch and rapped his knuckles on the front door.

He could hear a television on inside but saw no movement through the front door glass.

Knocking again, Evan called Burnham's name.

Maybe he's around back, he thought, descending the porch and striding to the back yard. "Mr. Burnham?"

When no answer came, Evan approached the glass sliding doors at the backside of the house.

He pressed his hands to the glass, his face moving in close. "Mr. Burnham?"

Surely, the man hadn't gone to sleep with the television blaring.

Evan jogged back to the front porch and knocked once more before trying the knob. The door wasn't locked.

"Mr. Burnham?" he called out with a bit more force, stepping inside. "Hello?"

Plucking up the remote, Evan muted the television, repeating the man's name as he slowly made his way through the house.

Evan stopped at the kitchen next, the putrid smell of rotted food suddenly assailing him.

He covered his nose, noticing an untouched steak and baked potato sitting on the bar, with a glass of wine a few inches to its right. A bad feeling settled in Evan's gut.

He tugged his cell phone free of the clip on his belt and put in a call to Donnie King. "Sheriff? It's Ramirez. I'm over here at William Burnham's place. Something's not right."

"How so?"

"Well, sir, his car isn't in the drive, but the television is on, and there's a rotted plate of untouched food on the bar in the kitchen. I've looked outside, and Burnham is nowhere to be found."

The sheriff cursed low. "Stay put. I'm on my way." He ended the call.

While waiting for the sheriff to arrive, Evan checked the attic and then the shed out back. But there was no sign of Burnham anywhere.

Moving back down the hall, Evan stopped outside what he assumed to be the master bedroom. The bed was unmade, but the rest of the room was neat as a pin.

He began opening drawers, only to discover Burnham's clothing neatly folded within.

Nothing seemed out of place, as if the man had simply driven off and not returned. Yet, if he'd been planning on leaving town for a while, he wouldn't have left the television on or the food sitting out on the bar. It just didn't line up with the rest of the house. The man was a neat freak if Evan had ever seen one.

Closing the drawers, Evan stepped inside Burnham's closet. A clear bin about the size of a shoe box sat on the shelf above his clothes.

Evan carefully retrieved it and carried it over to the bed.

He lifted the lid to find several old photographs, along with a handful of letters inside.

An attractive, dark-haired woman starred in most of the pictures, in several states of undress.

Evan flipped one over to discover some writing on the back. *Bill, I miss you every second of every day. Love, always. Alice. 1982.*

"Detective?" Donnie called out from the front room.

"In here, Sheriff."

Donnie appeared in the bedroom doorway. "Find anything?"

Evan shook his head. "Just some old photographs. Nothing that tells me where Burnham is."

The sheriff shook his head. "What is going on in my town, Detective? Three locals are missing, including the judge. Now Burnham?"

Evan dropped the picture back in the bin and replaced it where he'd found it. "I don't know, Sheriff. But I'm betting the answers can be found with Elijah Griffin."

"But what would Griffin want with William?" the sheriff asked, incredulously.

Evan shrugged. "Maybe he came here looking for incriminating evidence. You did say that Burnham had been investigating him."

"And Griffin seems to have skipped town," the sheriff growled. "I have an APB out on his truck. Hopefully, he'll turn up soon. In the meantime, I'm going to call the phone company and see if they can locate Burnham's cell phone."

The trill of the sheriff's own phone sounded overly loud in the otherwise quiet room. He unclipped it from his belt. "What ya got, Charlie?"

Evan watched the sheriff's expression change to one of shock. "What? Where?" And then, "We're on our way."

Donnie ended the call and met Evan's curious gaze. "One of the locals discovered a vehicle in Cutter's Pond over off Highway 2 while he was out there fishing."

Evan's heart picked up its pace. "What kind of vehicle?"

"He didn't say." Donnie turned to go. "I'll meet you out there."

Chapter Twenty

Evan stood in the afternoon heat on a hill at the top of Cutter's Pond, the sun beating down on his overly hot uniform.

He rested a hand over his eyes, watching an older model truck being winched from the water. "Any idea who it belongs to?"

Donnie nodded. "It's Hector's."

The sheriff had ordered the pond to be dragged in hopes of recovering a body. "I've got some guys coming from the next county over. If Hector is in that water, they should fish him out before nightfall."

Evan glanced at the pond, grateful that it wasn't overly large. "Hector's wife will need to be notified soon."

"Not until we find a body." Donnie shielded his eyes from the sun's glare and called out to Charlie.

The sweaty, overweight deputy strained his way up the hill from the water's edge, nearly losing his footing in the process. "Sir?"

"The detective and I just came from William Burnham's place. We found possible evidence of foul play. Take Deputy Calhoun out there with you and process the scene."

Charlie's brows shot up. "Foul play?"

"From the looks of his place," the sheriff muttered, "he left in a hurry and obviously didn't come back. His doors are unlocked, and an uneaten plate of food is rotting on his kitchen counter."

Charlie's splotchy red face paled. "That definitely doesn't sound like William. What do you think happened, sir?"

Donnie pinched the bridge of his nose. "I wish I knew."

"I think I have a pretty good guess," Evan interjected, drawing the attention of the sheriff and Charlie both. "After what I learned from Miss Caswell about Judge Powell, the prostitute, and Elijah, I'm willing to bet that Griffin is behind it all."

Charlie's eyes grew round. "Judge Powell and a prostitute? I'm not following."

Evan filled Charlie in on his conversation with Felicia Caswell. "I'm fairly certain that Elijah has been selling Elenore to the judge since she was eight years old. Maybe even younger."

It hurt Evan to say the words aloud, but that didn't make them any less real. "The prostitute, whoever she was, lined up the deals for Griffin."

Charlie only gaped in silence, so Evan continued. "If we dig deep enough, I'm betting that we'll find a connection between Griffin and the first three missing men of Wexler."

Finally finding his voice, Charlie rasped, "You're sure about Powell? I mean, he's been the judge in Wexler since I was born."

"I'm sure," Evan softly confessed.

"After you process William's place," Donnie began before touching Charlie on the arm to gain his attention, "swing by the Griffins' and feed that girl's animals. Do not disturb anything and do not go inside. Once that's finished, I want you back here to oversee the pond dragging."

Charlie blinked, seeming to digest everything the sheriff had told him. "Yes, sir."

Evan pulled a handkerchief from his back pocket and wiped the sweat from his forehead. "I'm going to see if I can catch Alan Brown's wife at home. Once I'm done questioning her, I'll stop by Dennis Baker's place as well as Hector's." He purposely left out that he planned on visiting Elenore that evening. But the sheriff didn't need to know that.

* * * *

Evan pulled into the drive of Alan Brown's quaint little home at the edge of town. A small white car sat in the open garage, telling Evan that Wanda Brown was most likely home.

He trailed up the yard and rang the doorbell.

A woman answered the door, wearing a robe, her bleached blonde hair pulled back in a ponytail. "May I help you?"

Evan noticed some mascara smeared beneath her eyes as if she'd been recently sleeping. "Mrs. Brown?"

"Yes. Are you here about Alan?"

"I am," Evan admitted, taking a step forward. "My name is Detective Ramirez. I was wondering if I could ask you some questions about your husband?"

She continued to stand there. "I don't know what I could tell you that I haven't already told Detective Burnham."

Evan didn't mention Burnham's disappearance. "I know, ma'am. But I've taken over for William Burnham since he retired, and I'd like to get caught up on your husband's case."

"Come in." She backed up to allow him entrance.

Once inside, Evan immediately noticed two things. Wanda Brown smoked in her home, and her cat's litterbox was full. He fought a gag.

"Have a seat, Detective."

Evan glanced at the dingy-looking couch. "I'm fine, Mrs. Brown. But thank you."

She shrugged. "Suit yourself."

Taking a seat in a sheet-covered recliner, Wanda lit up a cigarette and blew the smoke over her right shoulder. "Have y'all found out anything about Alan's disappearance?"

"No, ma'am. Not yet." Leaning a shoulder against the wall, Evan asked, "Did you ever hear your husband mention anything about Elijah Griffin?"

Wanda nodded. "He sold the piece of garbage one of our kittens a couple of years ago to help with their rat problems."

Evan let that sink in. "Is that all? Elijah never visited or called? Think, Mrs. Brown. It's important."

"Heck, I don't remember. Alan normally hung out at the Watering Hole. He didn't talk to me about much, and when he did, it usually involved his fists."

So, Alan Brown had been beating his wife. "What's the Watering Hole?"

"It's a bar over on 3rd Street. I'm surprised you haven't heard about it. The cops are always being called to that place."

Evan mentally filed that bit of information away. He opened his mouth to ask her another question when his gaze landed on a framed picture on the wall above the television.

He moved in closer to get a better look. A smiling Alan stood in the middle, one arm around Wanda and the other across the shoulder of the dark-haired woman that Evan had seen in the pictures in the bin at the top of Burnham's closet.

Nodding toward the photograph, Evan asked, "Who's the brunette standing between Alan and you?"

Wanda glanced toward the picture he indicated. "That's Alice Hastings."

Attempting to hide his curiosity, Evan casually remarked, "How long ago was that picture taken?"

Wanda snuffed out her cigarette and got to her feet, the smell of her smoke fairly choking Evan. "About five years ago. Why?"

"She just looks familiar," Evan smoothly lied.

"You wouldn't know her, Detective. She left here not long after that picture was taken. As far as I know, she hasn't been back."

Wanda took the photo down. A clean, white square remained on the nicotine-stained wall behind it. "She was the only friend I had in this godforsaken town."

"Do you still keep in touch with each other?"

Shaking her head, Wanda returned the picture to its place above the television. "No. She never returned my calls. Her phone was eventually shut off, or she changed her number. I'm not sure. Why the interest in Alice?"

Evan feigned indifference. "It's the detective in me. Just trying to get a feel of what Alan's life was like before his disappearance."

"Alice was my friend, not Alan's."

"They look pretty friendly in the photograph," Evan shot back, effectively angering Wanda.

She narrowed her eyes. "What are you implying. Detective?"

"I wasn't implying anything, Mrs. Brown. Just making an observation."

Thinking about the words on the back of the photo Evan had found in William's closet, he asked, "Was Miss Hastings involved with anyone that you know of?"

"She had a few dates here and there, but she wasn't serious with any of them."

Evan pierced her with a serious look. "What about Detective Burnham — did she date him as well?"

"Detective Burnham? I highly doubt it. Alice hated the law. She didn't have the best history where the cops were concerned."

That piqued Evan's curiosity even more. "Why is that?"

Wanda shrugged. "She was arrested a few times for some trumped-up charges that were eventually thrown out of court."

Of course they were, Evan thought, moving back a step when Wanda lit up another cigarette. "Do you happen to know where Alice moved to when she left here?"

"Birmingham. But like I said, she never returned any of my calls, so I couldn't tell you for certain."

Evan nodded, murmured his thanks, and trailed toward the door.

He stopped with his hand on the knob. "When was the last time you saw your husband, Mrs. Brown?"

"The afternoon before he disappeared." She followed him to the door.

Evan stepped out onto the porch to avoid the blast of putrid cigarette smoke. "Did he say where he was going when he left?"

She nodded. "The Watering Hole."

"Thank you, Mrs. Brown. I'll be in touch if I have any more questions."

"Sure thing." She closed the door behind him.

Chapter Twenty-One

Elenore sat in a chair across from Doctor Ingram, listening as he gently questioned her about her past.

"What do you remember of your mother?"

Mary Griffin's sad eyes flashed through Elenore's mind, vague in their familiarity. "I don't remember a lot about her, other than the fact she cried a lot."

"Because of your father?" the doctor prompted, writing something on a pad he held.

Elenore thought about that for a moment. "I don't know. Has Daddy been here to see me?"

Doctor Ingram paused in his writing. "Do you want him to visit you?"

She shook her head. "I— He won't be happy about me being in here."

The doctor crossed his legs at the knee. "Why do you think he'll be upset about you being in the hospital, Elenore?"

"He just will," she whispered, imagining how enraged he would be when he discovered where she'd gone.

"Tell me about your father."

Elenore swallowed, unable to meet the doctor's gaze. "He—He calls me Elle. Especially when I've displeased him."

"Elle, like the letter L?"

"Yes."

"And do you feel that you displease him a lot?"

Elenore hugged her middle. "I don't mean to. Daddy says I have something wrong with my brain that makes me do things he doesn't like."

Doctor Ingram wrote something on the pad he held. "What sort of things?"

She thought about the men that paid to visit her bedroom, and how her father would become irate if she cried or displeased any of them. But she couldn't tell the doctor that. He wouldn't understand.

When she remained quiet, the doctor pressed. "Elenore? What sort of things displeased your father?"

"If-if I didn't get the chores done on time or dinner finished before he got home, he would get angry."

"What happened when he became angry, Elenore?"

"He-he beat me."

The doctor continued to write. "What else did he do to you?"

Elenore's heart began to pound. Visions of her father holding her down while he took her violently skated through her mind, bringing nausea in their wake.

She recalled the first time he'd entered her room and climbed into her bed. She'd been only eight years old at that time, too young and innocent to understand what was happening to her.

But then the others began showing up...

"Elenore? Are you still with me?"

Doctor Ingram's voice brought Elenore out of her nightmarish thoughts. She nodded but kept her gaze averted.

"We'll come back to the question later. You mentioned that your father refers to you by the name Elle when he's upset with you. How does that make you feel?"

Elenore chanced a quick glance at the doctor before looking away once again. "It makes me feel dirty."

"Why do you think that is?"

"It's what Daddy calls me when I've been bad."

"I see. Did your father ever touch you in an inappropriate manner?"

The nausea was back full force. She didn't want to talk about her father. And she certainly couldn't tell the doctor what Elijah did to her when he drank. She couldn't betray him like that. No matter what, he was her flesh and blood, and he loved her. Didn't he?

Elenore shook her head.

The doctor laid his pen and paper aside. "According to your medical records, you've been in and out of the hospital for years with broken bones and several other injuries with different degrees of severities. Your father wasn't responsible for any of them?"

Elenore's breathing began to grow choppy. "I-I need some air."

"I can't help you if you don't talk to me, Elenore."

She jumped to her feet, finding it suddenly hard to breathe. "Please, Doctor, I need some fresh air."

Doctor Ingram stood as well. "Very well. We'll take a break for a while. Come on. I'll have the guard take you outside to the picnic tables."

Elenore rubbed her palms up and down her arms. "Thank you."

* * * *

"Detective?" More than a little surprised to see Evan Ramirez again so soon, Elenore sat up on her hospital bed and hugged her knees to her chest. "What are you doing here?"

Evan sent her a soft smile. "Just wanted to check on you and see how you're holding up."

Elenore thought about her session with Doctor Ingram earlier that day but decided not to mention it to Evan. He would think her crazy.

"The doctor says I'm getting better," she hedged.

"That's wonderful." Evan gestured toward a chair sitting next to her bed. "May I?"

"Yes."

He took a seat. "You look good, Elenore. Most of your bruising is gone, and you have a nice color back in your face."

Elenore wasn't sure how to react to the comment. No one had ever complimented her before. "Have you seen my father?"

Evan shook his head. "No one has, as far as I know. But we do need to find him. I was hoping you could help me with that."

"But I told you, Detective. I have no idea where he is."

"I know you did. But I thought that since you've had some time to rest and heal, maybe you'd recall something that might lead us to his whereabouts."

Elenore smoothed out the blanket covering her knees. "The last thing I remember was Daddy coming out of his room, holding his suitcase. He told me he was leaving town for a few days, and then he took all the cash from the cigar box on the mantle above the fireplace when he left."

"And he didn't say anything at all about where he was going?"

She shook her head.

Evan leaned back in his chair, his arms crossed over his chest. "Are you familiar with a woman named Alice Hastings?"

An image of a dark-haired woman with ruby-red lips appeared in Elenore's mind. "She was one of Daddy's friends."

Evan's arms slowly uncrossed. "So you knew her?"

"I only saw her a few times. She didn't come around a lot. But she used to stay the night with Daddy sometimes."

Elenore noticed the detective's eyes light up with interest. "So, they were in a relationship?"

A strong sensation of disgust overcame Elenore with the vision that question evoked.

She remembered Alice sitting on her father's lap in the corner of her bedroom, watching as Bill did unimaginable things to her. "If you want to call it that."

"Do you know where Alice is now?" Evan questioned, sitting forward in his chair.

Elenore shook her head, unable to remove the images of Alice and her father from her mind.

They had done things in that chair, despicable things while watching Bill hurt Elenore.

Meeting the detective's gaze, Elenore whispered, "I'd like to sleep now."

Chapter Twenty-Two

Evan drove back to Wexler, unable to get Elenore from his mind.

He couldn't seem to shake the feeling that she knew more about Alice Hastings than she'd let on. Like where the woman had relocated to. He'd be willing to bet if he could find Alice, he would also find Elijah.

But why would Elenore lie? Was she covering for her father? Evan couldn't imagine that being the case. It was more than obvious that she feared the man. Why then wouldn't she help law enforcement put him away?

Claire Lewis's words suddenly skated through Evan's mind. *"It's said that there's a strong indication that childhood abuse causes serious psychosocial development, leaving a wounded child within the adult they become. It's similar to Stockholm syndrome."*

Could that really be the case with Elenore? he wondered, parking along the curb in front of the sheriff's department. Was she so brainwashed by Elijah Griffin that she would die to protect him? Because if Evan didn't find the man soon, he feared that was exactly what would happen.

"Detective," Charlie greeted as Evan entered the building and headed straight for his office. "Did you have any luck with Wanda Brown?"

Evan slowed his steps, coming to a stop outside his office door. He turned to face the deputy. "Actually, I did. Have you ever heard of a woman named Alice Hastings? She lived here around five years ago."

Charlie nodded. "I arrested her a couple of times."

"On what charges?"

"Drugs and prostitution," Charlie simply stated. "The reason I recall it so vividly is because prostitution isn't something we see a lot of in Wexler."

Evan opened his office door and waved Charlie inside.

The deputy squeezed past him and took a seat in front of Evan's desk. "Why are you asking about Alice Hastings? I'm pretty sure she's been gone from this area for a number of years."

Taking a seat behind his desk, Evan booted up his computer. "When I was out at William Burnham's place, I discovered a box of pictures in the top of his closet. Alice Hastings was in one of those pictures. On the back it read, *Bill, I miss you every second of every day. Love, always. Alice. 1982.*"

Charlie's mouth dropped open. "William and Alice? But how — Why? He knew about her prostitution arrest and the drug charges the year before that."

"That's what I'd like to know, Charlie. I spoke with Elenore Griffin earlier today. She informed me that her father also had a relationship with Alice. And Wanda Brown had a framed picture of her on her wall, Alan and Alice in an embrace."

"Wow," Charlie muttered low. "I wonder if she had dealings with Hector Gonzalez and Dennis Baker, also?"

Evan thought about that for a second. "I'd be willing to bet she did. I'd also stake my life on the fact that Elijah Griffin is with her right now."

The phone on Evan's desk rang. He snatched it up while keeping his gaze on Charlie's stunned expression. "Ramirez."

The sheriff's voice came through the line. "Dennis Baker's vehicle has been found. Call

Charlie and have him meet you out on County Road 61 near Mabel Jenkin's farm. You'll see my car parked along the side of the road."

"Deputy Taylor is here with me, now, sir. We'll be right there."

Evan got to his feet and filled Charlie in on the sheriff's words. "I take it there wasn't a body found in Cutter's Pond?"

"No, sir, there wasn't." Charlie stood as well. "And no fingerprints on the truck, due to it sitting in the water for so long."

Evan skirted his desk and headed for the door. "Grab your processing kit and a couple more deputies and meet me out there."

"Yes, sir."

* * * *

Evan stood next to Sheriff King and watched Charlie and two more deputies process the scene. There'd been no evidence of blood in the vehicle or signs of a struggle. The car had simply been parked in a cornfield, the keys still in the ignition.

Evan's gaze scanned the scene before landing on the sheriff's profile. "How far is this from Elijah Griffin's place?"

"About two miles east of there, why?"

"So, close enough that Elijah could have driven the vehicle out here after disposing of Baker's body and then walked home in less than half an hour."

Donnie squinted in Evan's direction. "Cutter's Pond is approximately two miles west of the Griffin's place as well."

"I wonder if we would find Alan Brown's vehicle if we searched two miles to the south of Elijah's farm?"

The sheriff nodded. "I think it's worth a shot. In fact, you go south, and I'll look north. In the meantime, we have a temporary fill-in for Judge Powell. He came from the next county over. I'll put in a request for a search warrant on the Griffin place. Maybe we'll find something incriminating in that house."

Relieved, Evan asked, "Will you call me as soon as you hear back from the judge? I'd like to be there for the search."

"Of course." The sheriff tipped his hat and strode off in the direction of his vehicle.

Chapter Twenty-Three

Evan pulled his car off the side of the road, near the Wexler landfill. He tugged his cell phone free of its clip and put in a call to the station.

"Haverty County Sheriff's Department. This is Tom."

"Hey, Tom, it's Detective Ramirez. I need you to do something for me."

A brief pause ensued, and then, "Sure thing, Detective. What ya got?"

"Find out everything you can on an Alice Hastings. She was a longtime resident of Wexler before she relocated about five years ago. She's in the system, so any history on her will be easy to find."

"Alice Hastings. Got it."

Evan studied the entrance to the dump. "Get back to me with your findings as soon as you can."

"Will do."

After replacing the phone in its clip, Evan glanced both ways and then drove across the highway to the dirt drive.

The entrance to the dump was riddled with potholes and random pieces of trash.

A small building could be seen up ahead, perched in front of mounds and mounds of garbage.

Evan blew the horn.

The door to the building opened, and a stick-thin man stepped out, shielding his eyes from the sun.

Evan parked, switched off his vehicle, and got out. "Hey there. How are you?"

"Fine," the man answered, holding the door open to the building as if he'd been raised in a barn. "What can I do for you, Officer?"

Evan strode over and extended his hand. "I'm Detective Ramirez with the Haverty County Sheriff's Office. I was hoping to take a look around."

The guy accepted Evan's outstretched palm. "Sure thing, Detective. My name's Herman. What ya lookin' for?"

"A vehicle that doesn't belong here. You wouldn't happen to have seen anything suspicious out here, would you?"

"No, sir. But I'm normally inside in the air conditioning. You're welcome to look, though."

Evan glanced around. "How many acres of landfill you got here?"

"Oh, I don't own it. I just work here. But there's upwards of four hundred acres."

Great, Evan thought, eyeing the enormous piles of trash. How a small town such as Wexler could have so much waste was beyond him.

"You can take the golf cart if you'd like," Herman offered, reaching into the pocket of his jeans and pulling out a small set of keys. "It's got a full tank of gas."

Relieved that he wouldn't have to walk the four hundred acres, Evan accepted the keys. "I appreciate that."

Herman merely nodded and disappeared back inside the small building.

Evan made his way over to the golf cart and started the engine. It sounded like a well-oiled sewing machine.

He pressed the gas pedal and drove toward the mounds of garbage piles in the distance, wishing he'd worn something a bit cooler. It had to be pushing ninety-five degrees in the shade. *Great.*

An hour later, Evan returned empty-handed. There were no abandoned vehicles hidden on the property.

He thanked Herman once again and left the landfill, his stomach practically gnawing at his backbone.

"Any luck?" Evan asked Charlie, after placing a call to the deputy.

"No, sir. The only prints we were able to lift from Dennis Baker's car were his wife's and his. We found a couple of small sets all over the back windows and behind the seats, but they more than likely belong to his kids."

Evan inwardly sighed. "Any word from the sheriff?"

"Not yet. I take it you didn't have any luck at the landfill?"

"None," Evan wearily admitted. "I'm going to run by Gerald's Diner and have a late lunch. I haven't eaten today."

"Mind if I join you?"

Evan ground his teeth. He really didn't feel up to company. He simply wanted to eat in peace and then get back on the road in search of Alan Brown's and Judge Powell's vehicles. As well as William Burnham's. "Sure," he found himself saying instead.

Chapter Twenty-Four

Elenore sat on the bench of a picnic table at the rear of the hospital, watching two squirrels chase each other around the base of a giant oak tree.

She loved animals. Always had. They were the only creatures God created that hadn't hurt her in some way.

Of course, Evan had never harmed her, either. But she wouldn't allow her thoughts to dwell on the detective. He was, after all, a man. And men couldn't be trusted, no matter how nice they seemed at first.

The guard that normally accompanied Elenore on her outings tapped his watch, his silent way of letting her know it was time for her afternoon session with Doctor Ingram.

Elenore stood and strode back to the hospital, with the guard following closely behind.

After arriving at the entrance, he reached over her head and opened the door. "Watch your step."

Elenore thanked him and took the hallway to the right that led to Ingram's office.

"Come in and have a seat," the doctor offered the instant Elenore stopped inside the open doorway.

She cleared her throat. "Can we talk about something else today? Something besides my father?"

"We can talk about anything you'd like, Elenore."

With a slight nod, she moved deeper into the room.

The doctor sent her a smile meant to be reassuring. "Would you mind closing the door?"

Elenore glanced back the way she'd come. "I'd rather leave it open, if that's okay."

"If that's what you want."

"I do." She eased down into the chair and clasped her fingers together in her lap.

Doctor Ingram leaned back in his seat. "How are you feeling today?"

Elenore thought about that for a moment. "Better, I think. I was wondering when I could go home."

A small indention appeared between Ingram's eyes. "You're not here against your will, Elenore. You may leave anytime you choose to. Though, I wouldn't recommend it."

"But I'm better."

He reached across the desk and toyed with an ink pen lying there. "I want to show you something."

Elenore shifted in her chair, waiting while the doctor tapped on the keyboard of a computer on his desk.

He carefully turned the monitor toward her.

The screen lit up to reveal a video of Elenore, lying in bed, staring up at the ceiling without blinking.

Her face appeared unusually pale and sweat beaded on her forehead. "What is this?"

"It's you, Elenore."

"I know it's me, but why have I been videoed?"

He didn't respond. He merely tilted his head toward the screen, indicating she should keep watching.

Elenore reluctantly returned her gaze to the video in front of her. She watched in fascination as an orderly closed her blinds and tucked her in, all the while speaking to her in a gentle voice. Yet, she had continued to stare at the ceiling as if he were not in the room. "I-I don't remember this."

"I'm betting there are many things you don't recall or have blocked out, Elenore. Things you need to get past in order to heal."

Elenore shook her head, her stomach tightening, and her palms growing sweaty. "I don't understand. How can this be real?"

"Memories of traumatic experiences can hide deep in the brain, Elenore, causing psychiatric problems."

She flicked a glance in his direction before bringing her attention back to that video. "Psychiatric problems? Am I crazy?"

"No, Elenore. You're not crazy. Some bad experiences, such as childhood abuse, are so overwhelming and traumatic, the memories hide like a shadow in the brain."

He paused briefly. "Hidden memories that can't be consciously accessed may protect you from the emotional pain of reliving certain events. But eventually those suppressed memories can cause debilitating problems, such as anxiety, depression, PTSD, or dissociative disorders."

"PTSD?"

"Post-traumatic stress disorder," the doctor corrected.

Elenore's heart pounded hard enough she was certain he could see it beating through her clothes.

He continued to speak in a soft, comforting voice. "Something known as state-dependent learning is believed to contribute to the formation of memories that are inaccessible to normal consciousness."

Elenore didn't have a clue what any of that meant. She only knew that the person she was watching on that monitor looked like her, but it wasn't her. She had zero memory of anything taking place in that hospital room.

Turning her attention back to the doctor, Elenore whispered, "What's happening to me, Doctor Ingram?"

"Nothing we can't help you with, Elenore."

She twisted her fingers together in her lap. "What can you do?"

"There's a new drug available that I believe can help you access your memories — memories you've most likely suppressed. Coupled with hypnosis, I think we can bring those memories to the surface. There are two amino acids, glutamate and GABA, in the brain that control emotions and whether nerve cells are excited or calm. Under normal conditions, that system is balanced. But when we are hypersensitive, glutamate surges. Glutamate is also the primary chemical that helps us store memories to where they are easy to remember."

"What if I don't want to remember?" she asked in a quiet voice.

Doctor Ingram stared at her for long moments. "That's your right, Elenore. But if you truly want to heal, this is where it needs to begin."

Swallowing around the lump in her throat, Elenore consented. "Okay."

"We'll start in the morning, Elenore. Once you've had a good night's sleep."

Elenore's gaze drifted back to that monitor. "I'll be ready."

Chapter Twenty-Five

Evan sat behind his desk, looking over the information Tom had printed out on Alice Hastings.

She'd been arrested numerous times on drug charges and once for prostitution. Evan didn't recognize the name of the man she'd been arrested with. But he made a mental note to pay him a visit the following morning.

He glanced at the clock on the wall. It was half past six in the evening, which meant it would be dark soon.

The phone on his desk rang.

Snatching it up, Evan brought the receiver to his ear. "Ramirez."

"Hi, Detective, it's Tom in dispatch. We just got a call about an older model Chevy truck in the woods out on Calvin Ranch Road, about fifty feet from the intersection. If you're heading east, it'll be on your left. It matches the description of Alan Brown's vehicle. The witness is still out there."

"Notify Deputy Taylor. I'll call the sheriff."

"Already done," Tom admitted before hanging up the call.

More than a little exhausted, Evan pushed to his feet. He holstered his weapon and left the station.

For a small county of only 2415 souls, there sure was an awful lot of trouble abroad, he thought, climbing behind the wheel of his patrol car.

Evan started the engine and let his mind drift to Elenore.

He hated leaving her in a mental hospital. Especially alone without family or friends. Of course, with a family like hers, she was far better off alone.

Pulling away from the curb, he put in a call to the sheriff.

"This is King."

"Hey, Sheriff, it's Evan. Did dispatch notify you about the abandoned truck out on Calvin Ranch Road?"

Some rustling sounds came over the line. "Yeah. I'm getting dressed now."

"Charlie should be en route as well," Evan continued, turning onto the main road. "I'll see you there."

"Yep." The line went dead.

Evan blew out a breath and rubbed at the back of his neck. He had no doubt that Hector, Dennis, and Alan would eventually turn up dead.

He also wholeheartedly believed that Elijah was at the center of it all. He'd killed those men as surely as he had Judge Powell in his pocket. Well, *had* being the key word, Evan thought.

Powell would no doubt turn up dead as well. As would William Burnham.

But why would Elijah kill William now? Sure, Burnham had investigated the case of the missing men in Wexler, but he'd retired and no longer worked the case. It made no sense.

Unless Burnham knew something that Elijah didn't want brought out. Maybe he stumbled onto evidence that Elijah had used to blackmail Powell. Something to do with Elenore and the men Griffin sold her to.

Evan turned onto Calvin Ranch Road, the taillights of a vehicle reflecting in the distance.

He slowed to a stop behind the idling car and got out.

A middle-aged man approached, his hand extended in Evan's direction.

Evan accepted his outstretched palm. "I'm Detective Ramirez. Are you the one who called us about a truck in the woods?"

"Name's Ernie. And yessir, I was out scouting for a good spot to set up some coon traps when I ran across the truck. I recognized it instantly. It belongs to Alan Brown."

Evan nodded. "Wanna show me where you found it?"

Ernie turned toward the ditch. "Careful right there. There's places along here that are slicker than owl dung."

Evan grinned and followed Ernie through the ditch and into the woods beyond. "Do you know Alan Brown?"

"Course, I do. Everyone in town knows Alan. He practically lives at the Watering Hole. Well, he did afore he went missing."

The two of them trekked through the woods for a few minutes before Ernie stopped and pointed. "Right there."

Evan spotted the tailgate in the waning light. "I can take it from here, Ernie. Would you mind heading back out to the road and guiding the sheriff in when he gets here?"

"Sure thing. I sure hope y'all find Alan. He might not be the sharpest tool in the shed, but he was a likable enough fellow."

"We'll do our best." Evan carefully made his way toward the truck, already pushing Ernie from his mind.

Chapter Twenty-Six

"There's nothing to be nervous about, Elenore. We'll take it slow, and if it becomes too much for you at any point, we'll stop. All right?"

Elenore climbed onto the narrow bed Doctor Ingram had setup in the center of a solid white room.

The curtains were drawn on the windows, and the walls were devoid of pictures.

"I can see your curiosity," the doctor was saying, pulling a small table with wheels over next to the bed. "There are no pictures or paintings in the room for a specific reason. When doing hypnosis, we wouldn't want images on the wall to become part of your subconscious. The white is soothing, healing. It helps us to relax."

That made sense to Elenore.

Doctor Ingram retrieved a syringe from the small table, along with an alcohol wipe. "Are you ready to begin?"

At her nod, he opened the packet and swabbed her left arm. "This is the medication we talked about yesterday. It's going to make you feel a little sleepy, and you might experience a coldness in your limbs. Just remember, it's perfectly normal."

"Okay," Elenore whispered, her mind racing with anxiety.

"Try to relax."

The sting of the needle could barely be felt as he penetrated her with its tip. "There. All done."

He pulled a chair up next to her bed. "Now, let us begin."

Her eyes drifted shut.

* * * *

Pain. So much pain. Elenore lay on her bed, her back bowing with the white-hot agony running through her abdomen.

She looked down in horror, watching her sheets turn red with blood. "Daaaaddy!"

"She's going to bleed out," a feminine voice announced from nearby.

Elenore turned her head in the direction of that voice.

Alice Hastings paced along the side of the bed, wringing her hands and muttering something about prison.

"Will you just shut up?" Elijah snarled, thrusting a handful of towels in Alice's direction. "If you don't want her to bleed out, then do something."

Another pain ripped through Elenore, forcing a hoarse cry from her lips.

Alice snatched the towels from Elijah's hands. "If you had put her on the pill like I told you to, she wouldn't be miscarrying at fifteen years old! This is your fault. And if she dies, that's on you also."

Elenore's heart began to race. Was she losing her baby?

She reared up and looked over her slightly protruding belly at the massive amount of blood spilling from her body. "My-my baby."

"You better be more worried about yourself," Alice snapped, wadding up one of the towels and pressing it between Elenore's open thighs.

Alice sliced her gaze back to Elijah. "She needs a doctor!"

"No," he growled through clenched teeth. "No doctors. How in the world would we explain this? She's fifteen years old. They would throw us under the jail."

"Us? There is no us, Elijah. This is your doing. If you'd put her on birth control like I told you to, none of this would be happening."

Elenore attempted to breathe through her agony. Sweat ran down into her eyes as she lay in excruciating pain in the stifling hot room.

Elijah stepped forward, grabbing Alice around her throat. "You just do what needs to be done, or so help me God, I will bury you alongside her."

He shoved Alice away from him, storming from the room without so much as a glance in Elenore's direction.

Elenore's terrified gaze flew to Alice's face. "Help me."

Alice rubbed at her neck, snatched up another towel, and went back to work. "It'll be over with soon."

"My baby?" Elenore wheezed, gritting her teeth against the next pain slicing through her.

She didn't want her baby to die. It didn't matter how the child had been conceived or which man it belonged to. Elenore knew only that it was hers, and she would love it with everything she had.

"There is no more baby," Alice snapped, trying to stop Elenore's bleeding. "Now quit your talking and let me concentrate."

Elenore's heart shattered into a million pieces, the physical pain dulled by emotional devastation.

She stared up at the ceiling, tears leaking from the corners of her eyes. Her baby hadn't survived.

Grief unlike any Elenore had known before settled inside her. It wrapped around her in sickening finality.

She arched her neck, allowing the scream building there to burst free.

It went on forever, echoing throughout the room again and again.

Alice suddenly appeared in Elenore's vision, holding a syringe in her hand. "I can't have you fighting me."

The needle pierced Elenore's arm. Within seconds, blessed darkness descended upon her, a temporary reprieve from her grief and pain.

"Elenore?"

Somewhere deep in her mind, Elenore knew Doctor Ingram called to her, but she couldn't seem to escape the nightmare she found herself in.

"Look at me, Elenore. It's Doctor Ingram. You're all right now."

Focusing on the sound of his voice, Elenore fought through her grief, seeking the soothing comfort of his words.

"There you are," he murmured, tucking some hair behind her ear.

Elenore blinked, her watery gaze locking onto his face. "My baby. They killed my baby."

Doctor Ingram wiped her forehead with a cool, damp cloth. "Who killed your baby, Elenore?"

Nausea was instant. Elenore rolled to her side and vomited on the floor.

"It's okay," Doctor Ingram crooned before calling for an orderly. "Just breathe, Elenore."

The orderly arrived within seconds.

Elenore continued to gag, listening to the doctor speak in a low voice, ordering nausea medication and a cleanup crew for the vomit.

She lay there on her side, heaving through her pain—pain born of memories she'd suppressed all these years.

The nausea finally ebbed enough she could breathe without gagging.

She rolled to her back with the orderly's return, blocking out the needle he handed to Doctor Ingram.

The doctor administered the shot, his softly spoken words little comfort to Elenore's grief. "There. That should help."

Elenore looked up into his concern-filled eyes, unable to escape the memories swimming around in her head. "My baby died…"

Doctor Ingram studied her from behind his glasses. "How far along were you, Elenore?"

She strained to remember. "Five months, I think."

"And how old were you when you lost your baby?"

Elenore swallowed, her body beginning to relax from the medication Ingram had given her. "Fifteen."

Something akin to pity flickered in his eyes. Or maybe it was anger? She couldn't be sure.

"You were fifteen years old when you became pregnant? Do you know who the father of your baby was?"

Elenore shook her head. "There were so many visiting my room. I-It was my baby, Doctor Ingram. I was going to take her — if it was a girl — and leave with her."

The doctor continued to stare down at her. "Why were you planning on leaving if you'd had a girl?"

"So my father or any of the others couldn't hurt her like they did me."

"What others, Elenore?"

Elenore averted her gaze. "There were several besides my father. But Bill was the worst."

"Bill? Tell me about Bill."

The nausea threatened to come back, but she fought against it. "Bill hurt me more than the others. He wanted me to beg him to stop."

"And did you? Beg him to stop, I mean?"

Elenore stared at a small crack in the ceiling. "I used to until I learned how to escape him."

"How did you escape him, Elenore?"

She shifted her gaze back to the doctor. "I don't know. It just happened on its own. I learned how to block out what was happening to me, to hide in the white place."

The doctor wiped at her forehead once more. "The white place?"

"I don't know what the place was or how I got there. I only know that Bill couldn't touch me as long as I was there. None of them could."

"I see. When you say none of them could, you are referring to the others who hurt you?"

"Yes. There was more than one."

"And did you know the others who visited your room, Elenore?"

She slowly nodded. "I did…"

Chapter Twenty-Seven

"William Burnham's car has been located," the sheriff announced, stepping inside Evan's office the following morning. "And I got the search warrant for Elijah Griffin's place." He held up an envelope.

Evan met the sheriff's gaze. "Where was Burnham's car discovered?"

"A couple of miles south of Elijah Griffin's place."

"Why does that not surprise me?" Evan sarcastically muttered.

The sheriff shrugged. "Same reason it didn't surprise me, I reckon. We both know Elijah is guilty as sin. We just don't know to what extent."

Evan pinched the bridge of his nose. "Maybe we should call in the FBI on this. We could definitely use the help."

"Call them in for what, exactly?" The sheriff rested his hand on his hip. "The discovery of some missing vehicles? Until we start finding bodies, Detective, my hands are tied."

Evan's jaw tightened in frustration. He gestured toward the envelope the sheriff held. "I'd like to participate in searching the Griffin farm."

"That's exactly why I stopped here first. I remembered you wanted to be there for that. And I could sure use your help. I mean, Charlie is decent at his job, but sometimes he's like a bull in a china shop, if you know what I mean."

Evan was all too familiar with Charlie's lack of finesse. "Let's go."

The sheriff and Evan arrived at the Griffin farm a little more than ten minutes later. They parked along the dirt road, careful not to disturb any fresh tracks they might encounter.

"Doesn't look like anyone's been here recently," Donnie pointed out, sauntering up the drive.

Evan scanned the undisturbed dirt as well. "What about Charlie? Hasn't he been feeding the animals for Elenore?"

The sheriff nodded. "He has. But I told him to park along the road out there, so we could keep track of Elijah's comings and goings. That is, if we get lucky enough to catch him back out here. Which I highly doubt will happen."

"He'll come back," Evan stated with certainty. "He'll come for Elenore."

Donnie stepped up on the front porch and knocked, knowing full well there would be no one inside. "Sheriff's Department!"

Evan stepped up behind the sheriff and watched him try the knob. The door opened effortlessly.

Following the sheriff inside, Evan jerked his chin toward the hallway. "I'll start back there."

Donnie flicked his wrist in the direction of the kitchen. "I'll take the kitchen and living room."

Evan entered Elenore's bedroom a moment later. Her soft, clean scent bombarded him, leaving him weak in the knees.

He briefly closed his eyes and breathed her in before shaking off the sensation and moving toward her closet. He really needed to get over this strange attraction he had for her.

Studying the closet's contents, Evan took note of the meager dresses hanging inside. They were well worn and littered with stains.

There were no shoes present and no frilly girl items, such as purses and scarves. Apparently, the only pair of shoes she owned was the ones he'd bought her a few weeks ago.

Stepping in closer, he pulled down the two tattered blankets resting on the top shelf and ran his hand along its surface.

His fingers came into contact with something near the back corner.

He carefully took hold of it and brought it out. It was a picture of a beautiful blonde woman holding an infant in her arms.

Evan flipped the image over and read the writing on the back. *Mary and Elenore Griffin, 1999.*

Mary was smiling in the photo, a genuine-looking smile that reminded Evan of Elenore.

"What happened to you, Mary?" he whispered aloud, wondering what had caused her to run off and leave her daughter behind.

He put the picture back and covered it with the folded blankets. Apparently, Elenore hadn't wanted her father to know she had the photo.

Trailing across the room, he pulled open her nightstand, only to find it empty.

And then his gaze landed on the bed, the same bed he'd found her in weeks before.

The sheets hung half off the bed in a tangled disarray, exposing an enormous amount of dried blood on the stained-up mattress.

He recalled the moment he'd found her there, bloodied and beaten beyond recognition.

Rage and nausea came back, as powerful as it had the day he'd discovered her there.

"Christ," the sheriff breathed, stepping into the room. "Is that where you found Elenore?"

Evan could only nod, his gaze fixated on scene before him.

Donnie stopped next to him. "What's that under the edge of the bed by your foot?"

Evan backed up a step and dropped to his haunches. There, not three inches from his boot lay a bloody fireplace poker.

"Jesus," Evan growled through clenched teeth. "That has to be the weapon used to hurt Elenore with."

"I'll bag it. It could also be what was used on the missing men from town."

Evan hadn't thought of that. He couldn't think beyond what had happened to poor Elenore.

He pushed to his feet. "If you want to continue inside, I'll go have a look in the shed and barn."

Donnie touched him on the shoulder. "We'll find him, Detective."

Evan didn't respond. Partly due to the emotions swirling inside him and partly because he wasn't sure he believed the sheriff's words. Elijah Griffin was in the wind, and God knew how long it would be before the bodies of the missing men would be found. If ever.

Leaving the house by way of the back door, Evan strode out to the barn. His face felt overly hot. From the heat or his rage, he couldn't be sure.

The sounds of farm animals reached his ears the moment he stepped inside the old barn.

Stalls were situated along both sides, some housing an animal, some empty.

He stepped up to the stall containing the milk cow, noticing a tub of water and plenty of hay inside. Charlie was obviously doing a good job of keeping them fed.

Evan opened the stall door and stepped inside. "Hey there, girl."

After doing a quick sweep of the cow's stall, Evan moved down to the next one and then the next. But he found nothing suspicious or out of place in the barn.

The shed came next. Inside were shovels, rakes, and several other tools one would expect to find on a farm.

Sweat trickled down between his shoulder blades as he moved around the cramped space, looking for anything out of the ordinary. But he came up empty once again.

The sheriff appeared in the open doorway. "Any luck?"

Evan shook his head. "You?"

"Nothing. But I did bag the fireplace poker. I'm going to send it off to be analyzed."

Evan exited the shed, disappointed and growing angrier by the minute. "Elijah Griffin killed those men, Sheriff."

"I know." The sheriff appeared as weary as Evan felt. "Something will turn up. We just have to keep looking."

Evan closed the shed door. "I've got the Jefferson County Sheriff's Department looking for Alice Hastings. I'm betting if we find her, we'll find Griffin."

"I hope you're right, Detective. I hope you're right…"

Chapter Twenty-Eight

Elenore sat in her hospital room, staring out the window. She couldn't rid herself of the images plaguing her mind.

She'd lost her baby.

How could she have not remembered being pregnant?

According to Doctor Ingram, victims of extensive trauma sometimes suppressed memories as a coping mechanism. Had she really pushed the memory so far back in her mind, she'd forgotten about her unborn child?

Her head ached, and her eyes burned. But for some reason, she couldn't summon the tears that needed so badly to fall.

Elenore was broken—broken to the point where she no longer cared if she lived or died. In fact, dying was preferable over the emptiness threatening to drown her.

She couldn't get the sight of Alice wrapping her baby up in a towel and carrying it from the room out of her mind.

Elenore's vision dimmed the longer she sat, looking out that window. She forced her eyes to relax, attempting to escape inside her mind, to a place where nothing or no one could reach her.

"Elenore?" Evan whispered, bringing her back from the abyss.

She didn't want him there. She didn't want anyone there.

He appeared in her peripheral, lowering to his knees next to her. "How are you doing, Elenore?"

Keeping her gaze locked on that window, Elenore answered in a wooden voice. "I want to go home."

"But the doctor says he's making headway. Maybe give him a little more time to help you?"

That brought her attention down to his upturned face. "He can't help me, Detective. No one can."

Pity registered in his eyes. "Don't say that. Doctor Ingram is one of the best in his field. I believe he can get you on the path to recovery in no time, if you'll allow him to."

The room swam in Elenore's vision, bringing a feeling of panic in its wake. What was happening to her? "He tried some drugs and hypnosis on me yesterday. It brought out memories I'd suppressed—horrible memories I wish I could forget."

"Like what happened to you a few weeks ago?"

She shook her head. "No. Something that happened several years ago, when I was fifteen."

Evan stood and dragged a chair over next to her. He sat, half facing her. "Do you want to talk about it?"

She didn't, but the images were too raw not to. "The memories were so vivid, I can still feel them inside me, like they're clawing at my guts."

"What images, Elenore?"

Elenore swallowed with difficulty. "I was pregnant, Detective. How could I not remember my own baby?"

Evan stilled, his expression a mask of shock. "Pregnant? You have a child? I don't recall seeing that in your file."

"My file?"

His face reddened slightly. "I read the file Claire Lewis had on you when you went into foster care."

"That was before," Elenore whispered, turning to gaze out the window once again. "I was fifteen when I miscarried. My father and Alice disposed of my baby. I never even got to hold her."

The room shifted again, and a strange sensation filtered through Elenore. She couldn't seem to get enough air. "I don't feel so good."

Evan was on his feet in an instant. "What's wrong?"

"I-I don't know."

He quickly grabbed a washcloth lying on the sink in the room and wet it, before rushing back to her side. "Here. Hold this against your face while I go get some help."

Elenore accepted the cool cloth and pressed it tightly against her eyes.

She could hear Evan out in the hallway, calling for help.

An orderly rushed into her room. "What's going on with you, Miss Griffin?"

Elenore kept that cloth pressed to her eyes, her heart now pounding hard enough she could feel it thumping inside her chest. "I don't know. I can't breathe right, and my heart feels like it's going to beat out of my chest."

"She's having a panic attack," the orderly confessed to Evan. "I'll call the doctor."

"Elenore?" Evan softly called, his voice sounding close by. "Help is coming, okay? Just hang in there."

She could only nod, her anxiety overwhelming in its intensity. After all the years of abuse she'd suffered at the hands of so many, why would she break down now that she'd found a place of safety and security?

"What has happened?" Doctor Ingram questioned, bustling into the room. "Elenore?"

She wiped at her forehead with the cloth, her eyes still squeezed tightly shut.

Evan answered for her. "I think she's having a panic attack. She became pale and couldn't seem to catch her breath."

"This will help calm you," Doctor Ingram stated, stopping at Elenore's side. He lifted the sleeve of her gown, quickly giving her an injection in her upper arm.

Within seconds, Elenore's frantically beating heart began to calm.

"Breathe," Doctor Ingram softly ordered, rubbing his thumb along the injection site. "Slow, deep breaths. That's it."

Elenore's entire body relaxed under the medication. She continued to wipe at her forehead until she felt her mind regain some control.

Doctor Ingram rested his palm on her elbow. "Come on, Elenore. Let's get you in bed before the medication takes full hold. It'll help you sleep. And sleep is exactly what you need at the moment."

Elenore allowed the doctor to assist her from the chair and into bed. She lay on her side, watching the orderly in the room fill a paper cup with water and set it on the nightstand.

Her gaze drifted to Evan, noticing the worry swimming in his eyes. "Has my father been here?"

"No one's heard from him since before you went into the hospital," Evan quietly responded.

"Are my animals being fed?" Of all the things she wanted to say to him, that was all that came out.

He eased up next to the bed and took hold of her hand. "Yes, Elenore. Your animals are being fed and watered daily. Please don't worry about that. I promised you that I would see to their care, and I have."

Relieved, she fought to keep her eyes open. "Thank you, Detective."

Blessed darkness engulfed her.

Chapter Twenty-Nine

Evan followed Doctor Ingram from Elenore's room a few minutes after sleep had claimed her. "Is she going to be all right? I've never witnessed a panic attack before."

The doctor continued walking toward his office. "Unfortunately, panic attacks are something we see a lot of in here. They usually stem from the mind feeling out of control, unable to grab on to a single thought or emotion. It becomes overwhelming for the person experiencing it."

When Evan remained quiet, the doctor glanced over his shoulder and then stopped in the middle of the hallway. "Imagine being on a merry-go-round. It's spinning at a high rate of speed. Yet, when the ride stops, and you step off, your brain can't focus on any particular object. Everything around you continues to spin, even though your feet are planted firmly on the ground. It can be a terrifying experience if you don't know to expect that."

Evan's heart hurt for Elenore. He couldn't imagine the pain and suffering she'd endured all her young life — was enduring still. "She told me about the hypnosis — the miscarriage."

Doctor Ingram paused a moment longer, then entered his office. "Have a seat, Detective."

He waited for Evan to sit before lowering himself into the chair behind his desk. "As you know, I can't discuss Elenore's treatments with you, but since she's confided in you about some of it, I can say this. She's been abused to a point it won't be easy to come back from. Some patients never do."

Evan's gut tightened at the doctor's words. "But you feel that Elenore will? Come back from it, I mean?"

"It's difficult to say, Detective. It all depends on her and how strong her will to survive is."

Evan let that sink in. "Still no sign of her father?"

The doctor shook his head. "No, thank God. I fear seeing him right now might just be what pushes that girl on over the edge. If she's not already there."

Evan feared the same.

* * * *

"Detective?"

Evan looked up from the file he'd been going over since arriving back at the station, to find Charlie standing in the open doorway to his office. "Deputy Taylor. Come in."

Charlie entered the room and dropped his weight into the chair in front of Evan's desk.

"We just heard back from the Jefferson County Sheriff's Department. Alice Hasting's last known address didn't pan out. Apparently, she up and left in the middle of the night several years ago, owing a hefty sum of money to the landlord."

Evan rubbed at his aching forehead. "No one has any idea where she went? I mean, what about friends or a significant other?"

Charlie shrugged. "The landlord said she never saw anyone there but Miss Hastings. Apparently, she didn't have any friends. The landlord also said Miss Hastings worked at a local bar in town, toting drinks, but when she went there looking for her about the rent owed, they said Miss Hastings never showed for her shift, and they haven't heard from her since."

"How long ago was that?"

Charlie pulled a small pad from his right breast pocket and flipped it open. "A little over four years ago."

"Wherever she is," Evan sighed in a weary voice, "you can bet the farm that Elijah Griffin is with her."

Charlie got to his feet and started toward the door. He paused with his hand on the knob and looked back at Evan. "How is Elenore doing?"

"Not good. She's been through a lot for one so young. In fact, she's been through more than most could dream up in their worst nightmares. I just pray the doctors over there can help her."

"Yeah, me too."

Once Charlie left, Evan stood and closed the folder in front of him. He made his way through the station and out the front door, taking a right toward Gerald's Diner that lay one block ahead.

The diner was abuzz with customers having an early dinner when Evan stepped inside.

"Detective," Minnie boomed, rushing past him with two plates in her hands. She deposited them on a nearby table and then hurried back to his side. "Sit wherever you can find a clean table. It's been busier than a runover dog chasing a loose hubcap around here this evening."

Evan strode to the bar and took a seat next to Mabel Jenkins, who seemed to be engrossed in a crossword puzzle. "Howdy, Mabel."

"Detective," she muttered without looking up. "Been a bit since I've seen you in here. Where ya been?"

Evan ordered a glass of tea from Gerald, who was busy on the giant grill behind the bar, before answering Mabel. "I've been investigating the missing persons cases."

"Y'all catch Elijah Griffin yet?"

"Not yet." Evan took a sip of his tea.

Mabel laid her pencil down and raised her gaze. "You ain't gonna find him until he wants to be found. He's a crafty old coot, that one. Probably holed up out in them woods near his farm. Have y'all checked out there?"

Evan shook his head. "I don't know my way around here that well. What makes you think he's hiding out in the woods?"

"Just a hunch. He was always in them woods, doing lord knows what. I know he made moonshine out there for years, but I ain't heard much about it in a long time. Folks around here grew tight-lipped after that trial took place. I reckon they were scared of him. Course, I don't blame 'em. I'm half afraid of him myself."

Evan put in his order, listening to Mabel talk about everything from coon hunting to knitting a blanket for her grandson.

His burger and fries arrived a few minutes later. He picked up a French fry and popped it into his mouth, his mind swirling with Mabel's words. Elijah had a place in the woods behind his house where he'd once made moonshine.

Evan bit into his burger next, his eyes nearly rolling back in his head. That had to be the best burger he'd ever tasted.

He swallowed and faced Mabel once more. "What else can you tell me about Griffin?"

Sharp as a tack, she lifted her gaze, her eyes narrowed. "I believe he killed his wife Mary."

That caught Evan off guard. Although, it shouldn't have. After everything the man had done to his own daughter, Evan believed Elijah capable of anything. "What makes you think he killed his wife?"

"Just the way everything went down. Mary was a sweetheart. A beautiful girl full of life. Until she married that piece of trash, Elijah.

Afterwards, she became distant, stopped coming into town as much. Then she had Elenore, and that baby became her whole world. She wouldn't have left that youngin behind, Detective. She just wouldn't have."

The anger that had been festering inside Evan since taking on the case, boiled to the point where he lost his appetite.

He pushed to his feet and dropped a twenty-dollar bill on the bar. "Thank you, Mabel. You've been a huge help."

"Yep," she responded, picking up her pencil and jumping back into her crossword puzzle.

Evan sent a nod to Minnie and hurried from the diner. He had some research to do — research involving Mary Griffin and the man she'd supposedly run off with. He also planned on scouting the woods surrounding the Griffin farm. With any luck, he'd catch Elijah out there.

Or at the very least, find evidence of the missing men in town.

Chapter Thirty

Elenore sat in the hospital cafeteria, a plastic fork in hand, aimlessly pushing her food around on her plate. She had no appetite, hadn't since her hypnosis session with Doctor Ingram a few days ago.

He'd kept her mildly sedated, which seemed to help a little…but not enough. Not nearly enough.

Her mind felt empty, save for the bouts of nausea she experienced, reliving her miscarriage.

Chunks of her life were missing, she numbly realized. Which wasn't a bad thing, considering her traumatic past.

Sensing someone's approach, she looked up in time to see Doctor Ingram stop in front of her table.

"Hello, Elenore." He gestured to the chair he stood next to. "May I?"

Elenore simply stared up at him, unable to summon the energy to nod.

"Okay then." He pulled out the chair and took a seat. "How are you feeling today?"

"Empty," was all she could manage.

Sadness reflected in his eyes. "It's to be expected when one delves into traumatic memories—memories their minds have protected them from. It'll get easier the more you purge them, Elenore."

"I don't want to purge anything else, Doctor. Not for a long time, anyway. If ever."

Ingram pushed his glasses up on his nose. "I understand your reluctance. But if we stop now, it could take years for you to fully recover. If you ever do."

Elenore didn't care. She wanted to forget what her session with Doctor Ingram had conjured up, forget what her father had done, forget Alice and Bill and all the others who had hurt her.

She held the doctor's gaze. "I want to go home."

"Elenore, please think about what you're saying. You're safe here. I— We, the hospital, will do everything in our power to see to your safety and mental wellness. Give us a chance. Don't give up after one treatment. Please."

Something, no matter how minute it was, sparked to life at the doctor's words. Deep down, Elenore wanted to believe him, wanted to believe he could help her live a normal, healthy life. But she couldn't. Try as she might, she couldn't find the optimism to buy into his speech. So, she said nothing.

The doctor continued to watch her, as if expecting her to relent.

When she remained quiet, he blew out a defeated breath. "Will you at least take a few days to think about it? And then if you still want to leave, I'll work on your release paperwork so the state will cover your time here, as well as any medications you'll need to be on after your release."

The doctor was trying his best to help her. Somewhere deep inside, she knew that. Yet she couldn't summon the proper emotions she should be feeling. Emotions such as gratefulness or appreciativeness. The normal emotions one would feel. But she felt nothing other than emptiness. And nausea. Always with the nausea.

Elenore pushed her plate away and moved to stand.

Dizziness was instant. The room spun in her vision, sending more nausea slicing through her.

"Elenore?"

She could hear the doctor's voice coming from far away.

The room continued to spin until she could take no more. Her world turned to black.

* * * *

Elenore awoke to find a strange man peering down at her.

She instinctively scrambled back, her heart kicking up a notch.

"You're awake," he unnecessarily pointed out. "My name is Doctor Carson. Do you know where you are, Miss Griffin?"

Elenore's gaze swept her surroundings. It took her a second to realize she was in an emergency room. She glanced down at her arm to find an IV inserted there. "Why am I in the ER?"

"You fainted and hit your head. Doctor Ingram had you brought here for fear you'd had a concussion. Thankfully, you don't."

Elenore slowly pushed herself up against the pillows of her temporary bed, warily watching the doctor jot down notes in what she assumed to be her chart.

He spoke while continuing to write. "How far along are you in your pregnancy, Miss Griffin?"

Elenore's heart stopped. She'd misunderstood him. He couldn't have possibly said what she thought. "I—I'm not…"

"Pregnant?" he finished for her, hanging her chart on the end of her bed. "High levels of HCG, or human chorionic gonadotropin, showed up in your blood work. You're most definitely pregnant."

What little bit of sanity Elenore had been clinging to so tightly threatened to slip away in that moment.

She brought a trembling hand to her mouth in an attempt to hold back the vomit rapidly making its way north.

Doctor Carson handed her a pink tray and quickly disappeared on the other side of the curtain surrounding her bed.

Minutes ticked by before a young, dark-haired nurse rushed into the room, wearing gray scrubs and a matching gray scrunchie in her hair.

She administered some medication into Elenore's IV. "There. It shouldn't take long to kick in. It'll help to ease some of your nausea."

The nurse thankfully discarded the half-full pink tray and handed Elenore a clean one. "Just in case."

Elenore wanted to die—to just close her eyes and never wake again.

She accepted the tray and held it close to her mouth.

"My name's Kate," the nurse informed her while adjusting the IV equipment. "If you need anything, just press that button hanging on the bedrail by your head. I'll be here taking care of you the rest of the night."

Elenore dropped her head back against the pillow. "I'm staying overnight?"

The nurse nodded. "The doctor thinks it's best, considering your condition. Do you know how far along you are?"

"I didn't even know I was pregnant," Elenore whispered, her body relaxing from the nausea medication.

Kate sent her a reassuring smile. "It happens."

Against one's will, Elenore thought, her mind racing with the implications of a pregnancy. She had no idea who the baby belonged to, and even if she did, she wouldn't want them to know.

Memories of her long-ago miscarriage assailed her in that moment. No, she couldn't let them know.

Chapter Thirty-One

Evan walked alongside Charlie through the woods behind the Griffin farm. "How much land does Elijah have out here?"

"Something like sixty acres," Charlie answered, stepping over a patch of briars. "If you ask me, he should have sold some of it years ago and fixed up that house of his. It looks like it's on its last leg."

Evan continued walking, his gaze touching on everything around him. "How much further is that moonshine still?"

"Not far. Just up ahead through those trees."

A minute later, the two of them broke through the trees to find an old moonshine still.

Some kind of a large cast iron contraption, with what appeared to be copper tubing coming out of the top, rested in front of a rundown shack. A big pot that reminded Evan of a pressure cooker sat to the left of the cast iron contraption. "I take it this is where the moonshine was made."

"Yep." Charlie stalked toward the shack. "This is where he stored the jars and ingredients used to make the shine."

"Be careful." Evan unholstered his 9mm and followed Charlie to the shack's door. "We don't know what or who's in there."

Charlie freed his weapon as well, crept closer, and jerked open the door.

A possum came charging out, nearly giving Evan a heart attack. Charlie, too, if his expression were any indication.

"Christ," Charlie hissed, his breathing accelerated. "I about peed myself."

Evan stepped up to the opening, his 9mm entering the room ahead of him.

"It's clear," he informed Charlie while holstering his weapon.

There was nothing remarkable on the inside of the cabin. Cobwebs hung in all four corners of the space, and a few broken jars were perched along the shelves on the wall.

"It doesn't look as if he's been here," Charlie unnecessarily announced, stepping in behind Evan. "I didn't see any tracks outside, either."

"Neither did I." Evan searched the floor of the shack, on the off-chance Elijah had buried something or someone there. But the earth beneath his feet was hard and undisturbed.

Stepping back outside, Evan turned to face Charlie. "Why don't you head west, and I'll go east. We can cover a lot more ground that way. It's going to be dark soon, and I sure don't want to be caught out here once the sun goes down."

"I feel ya." Charlie spun on his heel and strode off in a westerly direction.

Evan glanced at his watch and then called out to Charlie's retreating back. "We'll meet up at the car in one hour."

Charlie's right hand flew up, telling Evan without words that he heard and understood.

Evan traipsed around the area, checking behind the shack and the surrounding tree line before striking out to the east.

Nothing appeared disturbed along the ground, and no tracks of any kind could be detected.

More than a little dejected, Evan made a wide sweep and turned back toward the shack.

A shot rang out in the distance, spurring Evan into a dead run. *Charlie!* He unholstered his weapon as he ran.

Every scenario Evan could imagine ran through his mind at once. Had Elijah caught Charlie on his property? Had Charlie stumbled onto the deranged maniac without knowing it?

Evan ran faster.

He wanted to call out to the deputy, but he refrained. If Griffin were out here, Evan would need the element of surprise on his side.

He sailed over a palmetto bush and nearly slammed into Charlie in the process.

"Jesus Christ, Charlie! I like to have shot you." He holstered his weapon.

The deputy simply stood there, holding an extremely long rattlesnake by the tail. Blood dripped from the serpent's head to speckle the dirt at Charlie's feet. "He nearly got me."

Evan half bent, resting his palms on his knees, attempting to get his breathing under control. "You scared the crap out of me, Deputy."

"Oh, the gunshot," Charlie sheepishly replied. "Sorry about that, but it was either me or him. I had no choice."

Evan jerked his chin in the direction Charlie had come from. "Well, if Griffin was out here, he's not any longer."

Charlie tossed the snake into the bushes. "I take it you didn't find anything suspicious either?"

"No. We might as well head on back." Evan straightened and made his way back in the direction of their cars.

Charlie quickly caught up with him. "Where do we go from here, Detective?"

Evan glanced at Charlie's profile. "I'm going to the station to try to piece together what I can on this case. My biggest priority is locating Elijah Griffin. And to do that, I need to find Alice Hastings."

"What if she's dead, too?"

Evan slowed his steps. "What do you mean *too*?"

Charlie shrugged. "You know as well as I do that those missing men in town are dead, Detective. It doesn't take a rocket scientist to figure that out."

"True. But until we find some bodies, they're still considered missing. No matter what we think we know."

"Maybe we should call in for outside help."

Evan grunted. "I've already suggested the FBI, but the sheriff shot that idea down. And technically, he's right. We can't just call in the feds for some missing people."

Charlie remained quiet for a moment and then said, "There was a case in Mississippi where the feds were called in on two missing children."

"I know, Charlie. But the sheriff is the only one who can make that call. And apparently he's not ready to do that."

Evan and Charlie walked the rest of the way back to their vehicles in silence.

Once Evan reached his car and unlocked the door, he peered at Charlie over the top. "Why don't you head back out to Judge Powell's place and speak with his wife once more. Dig back as far as you can with her. She may be hiding something."

Charlie nodded. "Sure thing. I'll catch up with you back at the station."

Sliding behind the wheel of his car, Evan started the engine and waited for Charlie to pull away. He laid his head back against the seat, staring out his windshield at the rapidly descending sun. *Where are you, Elijah?*

Chapter Thirty-Two

"The ambulance is here to give you a nonemergency transport ride back to Flagstaff," a blonde nurse announced, stepping into Elenore's hospital room, holding some items in her hands. "I'll get that pesky IV out of your arm first."

Elenore stared straight ahead. "I'm not going back to Flagstaff."

"But—"

"I'm going home," Elenore interrupted, cutting off the rest of the nurse's words.

The blonde simply stood there for long moments. "Okay. I'll need to notify your mental health physician and see what he wants you to do."

Elenore sliced her gaze in the nurse's direction. "It doesn't matter what he wants. I wasn't court ordered to be there. I can leave at any time. And I choose to leave now."

The nurse's expression blanked. "All right then. Do you have someone coming to pick you up?"

Shaking her head, Elenore quietly stated, "Not yet, but I'll find someone."

Pity flashed in the blonde's eyes. She eased up next to the bed and placed the items she held on the edge of the mattress. "Very well."

Elenore lay there quietly while the nurse removed the IV from her arm, trying to decide if she wanted to call the detective to pick her up.

"There. All done," the blonde announced, properly disposing of the IV needle. She taped a bandage over the bruised injection site and turned to go.

"Wait." Elenore cleared her throat. "Can you get me the number to the Haverty County Sheriff's Department?"

A small indention appeared between the nurse's eyes, but thankfully she didn't question Elenore's request. "Sure thing."

"Thank you." Elenore watched her go, her mind still reeling from the bomb the doctor had recently dropped on her.

She lowered her gaze to her flat stomach, her brain too numb to fully comprehend her situation.

The anxiety crept in without notice, bringing the dreaded panic in its wake.

Elenore had been too young to fully understand the implications when she'd become pregnant at fifteen. But she wasn't too young now.

More panic flooded her system. Breathing became difficult, and the room spun in her vision.

She squeezed her eyes tightly closed as images from her past began to tunnel through her once again.

Memories of her mother's smiling face bombarded her. Her laughter, her tears...

Elenore practically jumped from the bed, wearing a hospital gown and nonskid socks.

She rushed from the room only to end up disoriented in the hall.

"Miss Griffin?" a nurse called out from behind a large, horseshoe-shaped desk. "Are you okay?"

Elenore couldn't seem to focus on her face, so great was her panic.

"Hey! Miss Griffin?"

The nurse surged to her feet and strode in Elenore's direction. "What's wrong, Elenore? Talk to me."

The woman's voice sounded as if it came from a great distance. Elenore tried to focus on her words, but her brain had other ideas.

Darting around the nurse, Elenore ran, her gaze touching on dozens of doors lining the hall.

An exit sign suddenly came into view.

Elenore turned in the direction of the sign, nearly running into a patient holding on to a walker.

Tears began to spill from her eyes, so great was her fear. Her heart felt as if it would burst from her chest, and her entire body broke out into a sweat. Still, she ran.

She bypassed the elevators, unable to stop her panic long enough to wait for the doors to open.

Bursting into the stairwell, Elenore flew down the stairs until she found herself at the last door.

She pushed it open, relieved to see the parking garage.

"Hey, lady, are you all right?" a man asked from a short distance away.

Elenore ignored him. She broke into another run until she exited onto the street beyond.

Down the sidewalk she went as dozens of faces blurred by in her peripheral. She had no idea where to go, no idea where she was, and definitely no clue how to get home.

She had no money, no clothes, and no phone.

A soft whimper echoed around her. It took a moment for her to realize it came from her.

She suddenly slammed into something, nearly knocking what little breath she had from her lungs.

"Easy," a man crooned, his powerful arms going around her. "I got you."

Elenore went wild with fear. Someone had grabbed onto her. She couldn't breathe, couldn't think.

His breath hissed next to her ear as she sank her teeth into his shoulder.

"Calm down, lady! I'm only trying to help you."

Elenore fought until she could fight no more. Exhaustion took over, leaving her weak and panting.

The man's arms remained around her for long moments before he finally released her. "There, now. It's gonna be okay. Everything's all right."

Elenore began to shiver, her teeth chattering behind her lips. She attempted to focus on the man standing in front of her, but her mind wouldn't calm enough to comprehend. "W-where a-am I?"

"You're in Montgomery. Did you just come from the hospital a few blocks over?"

She could only nod, the sounds of horns blowing and engines revving swirling around in her scrambled brain.

"I take it you bailed?"

When she didn't answer, he took hold of her hand. "Come on, let's get you off the street before you get hit by a car."

Elenore didn't care. Voices—so many voices—were whispering through her mind. They blended together until she couldn't follow along.

Her hands flew up to the sides of her head. "Please, make it stop."

"You must be detoxing," the man murmured, sweeping her up into his arms. "Well, I have just the thing to fix that."

Somewhere deep inside Elenore, she knew she should break free and run from this man. But she couldn't bring herself to resist.

She wasn't sure how long he walked with her in his arms before he entered a dimly lit hallway. He strode ahead a few more feet, opened a door, and carried her across the room.

"Just relax," he insisted, placing her trembling form on a bed by a window. "I'm gonna hook you up with the good stuff. You'll be better in no time."

Elenore lay there, unable to focus on anything in particular, her heart still pounding painfully.

The man returned, wrapping something around her upper arm, tight enough it pinched. She didn't care. Nothing mattered in that moment but escaping the panic going on inside her.

Another pinch, and then blessed warmth. Her body began to warm from the inside out. Her teeth stopped chattering, and her mind slowed its kaleidoscope of images and voices.

The man's face appeared in her line of sight. She noticed he had dark hair and green eyes similar to Evan's.

He leaned in close. "Sleep now. You'll be better when you wake up."

Elenore didn't want to sleep. She felt vulnerable and afraid. Yet her eyes drifted shut, regardless, until blessed sleep finally claimed her.

Chapter Thirty-Three

Evan awoke to the sound of sirens. He sat up, rubbing the sleep from his eyes, and trailed over to the window facing the street beyond.

Yawning, he made his way to his small kitchen, switched on his police scanner, and started the coffee pot.

According to the scanner, there was a motor vehicle accident at the intersection of County Road 2 and Highway 31.

Evan pushed the incident from his mind and sauntered into the bathroom to shower.

After stripping and turning on the water, he stepped under the hot spray and thought about Elenore. He would go visit her today.

Evan had spent half the night at the station, going over every piece of information he could find on Elijah Griffin. From Alice Hastings to Judge Powell and the three missing men from

Wexler. But why would Elijah want to kill William Burnham? That one bothered Evan the most. There were no ties between the two men. Unless Burnham had discovered something about Griffin that could take him down.

Turning off the shower, Evan quickly dried himself and returned to his bedroom to get dressed.

His cell phone lay on the nightstand next to his bed, showing he had a missed call.

Odd, he hadn't heard it ring. Of course, he'd had the ringer off while he'd gone over dozens of files.

He swiped his finger across the screen, recognizing Doctor Ingram's number.

His stomach tightened in dread. Doctor Ingram wouldn't be calling him unless something was wrong with Elenore.

Zipping up his pants, he sat on the edge of the bed, pulled on his shoes, and dialed Doctor Ingram.

"Ingram," the doctor answered on the third ring.

"This is Evan Ramirez. I just saw where you'd tried calling me last night."

The doctor sighed through the line. "Elenore Griffin is gone."

Evan's heart flipped over in his chest. "What do you mean she's gone?"

"I had her transported to the nearest emergency room. They kept her overnight for observation. From what I gathered, she ran while the nurse was gone to grab her discharge papers."

Evan couldn't believe what he heard. "She ran?"

"I'm afraid so. From what I've been told, she literally ran from the hospital, nearly mowing down a few patients on her way out."

That didn't sound like Elenore to Evan. "Why was she sent to the ER?"

"I'm sorry, Detective, you know I can't—"

"You can't tell me. I know. How long has she been gone?"

"Since yesterday."

Evan ground his teeth. "I'll go by the farm and see if she's there. If she contacts you in the meantime, let me know as soon as possible. Otherwise, I'll be at Flagstaff in an hour and a half." He ended the call.

Pouring his coffee into a Styrofoam cup, Evan brushed his teeth and hair and hurried from his apartment. He would just have to grab breakfast at the nearest drive-thru he came to.

The drive to the Griffin farm was uneventful, giving Evan time to mull over the doctor's words. Elenore had run from the hospital.

None of it made any sense to Evan. Elenore had been through some bad stuff in her life, but she didn't strike him as the type to run.

Of all the trauma she'd experienced over the years, and survived, why would she run now, when she was finally getting the help she so desperately needed? It made no sense.

He pulled along the edge of the dirt road in front of the Griffin place, being sure to check for evidence of whether or not Elijah had returned. But there were no fresh tracks in the drive leading up to the house.

Careful not to disturb the earth around him, Evan made his way along the grass that led up to the front porch.

He rapped his knuckles on the door, listening for evidence of someone inside. He wanted so badly to bust through that door and search the house. But of course, he couldn't.

The previous search warrant they'd been granted was only good for that one search. To enter that house again, he would need to request a new warrant. And that would take time, even if the judge decided to grant him one. Which he doubted would happen.

When no answer came, Evan jumped from the porch and looked through a window on the side of the house. There were no lights on, no television playing in the background. "Elenore?"

Silence.

More than a little frustrated, Evan strode around back to the barn. "Elenore?"

A couple of goats responded to his voice, but other than that, there were no signs of Elenore anywhere.

* * * *

Evan sat in a chair in Doctor Ingram's office, watching the man clean the lenses of his glasses before perching them back onto his nose.

"Why was Elenore sent to the emergency room?" Evan questioned the doctor in a serious tone. He wanted answers, and the man sitting in front of him was the only one who could give them.

Ingram blew out a breath. "You of all people, Detective, should know that I can't answer that. Suffice it to say, she needed medical attention immediately. I did what I felt was best for her. And that was to have her transported to the emergency room where she could get the care she needed."

"I'm not asking you to hand me her medical records, I'm asking you to help me find her. And the only way I can do that is for you to tell me why she was sent to the ER."

Doctor Ingram leaned back in his chair and studied Evan for long moments. "Patient confidentiality—"

"I don't want to hear that," Evan barked, rising to his feet. "She's not well, Doctor Ingram. If she's on the streets, God knows what will happen to her. Do you want that on your conscience? If she dies, it's on you."

The doctor wearily stood. "Look, I can't divulge any details about Miss Griffin." He cut his eyes toward the folder lying on top of his desk. "However, I'm going to the cafeteria for a cup of coffee. If you would like to wait here for me, I'll be back in ten minutes."

Evan knew exactly what the doctor was getting at. He intended to give Evan ten minutes alone with that folder…Elenore's folder.

It couldn't have been an easy decision for Ingram to make. He'd probably never done anything unethical in all his years as a doctor.

And if Elenore's life were not in danger, Evan doubted the man would be helping him now.

"Thank you, Doctor."

Ingram didn't acknowledge his words; he simply strode around the desk and left the room, pulling the door shut behind him.

Evan reached across that desk and snatched up that file. He quickly read through the doctor's notes on Elenore's hypnosis, and his teeth clenched in anger. The details of her miscarriage were laid out before him.

Evan made a decision in that moment. He would kill Elijah Griffin when he found him. And he would find him. No matter how long it took or how far he had to travel to reach the man. Evan had a bullet with Elijah's name on it.

Reading further, he came to the doctor's notations on the day that Elenore was transported to the emergency room. *Patient presented with anxiety, dizziness, and nausea.*

Words like *fainted, possible concussion,* and several more details were jotted down on the page. But that wasn't what caused the blood to drain from Evan's face. There, on the bottom of the page was the word *pregnancy.*

Evan continued to read, but he couldn't get that word out of his mind. The emergency room had determined that Elenore was with child. But how? Evan wondered, his mind racing with images of poor Elenore walking down that dirt road, her shoes held together by duct tape.

It took a moment for him to realize he had tears swimming in his eyes, tears of rage and helplessness. Elenore's unborn child more than likely belonged to her father.

Evan felt sick. He closed the folder and staggered from Ingram's office.

"Detective?" Ingram called out, heading back down the hall with a coffee cup in hand. "Are you all right?"

Evan swallowed back the string of curses that threatened to spill forth. "How far is the hospital from here, where you sent Elenore?"

"Nine, maybe ten minutes. Jump on the interstate and head south to exit 63. It's approximately a mile up on the right once you exit."

"Thank you, Doctor," Evan quietly proclaimed.

Ingram took a sip of his coffee. "For what?"

"For everything."

The doctor moved to enter his office. "I'm sure I don't know what you're talking about." He closed the door behind him.

Evan hurried down the hall, taking the elevator to the bottom floor. He exited the hospital and jogged the rest of the way to his car.

Sliding behind the wheel, he started the engine and drove to the main road that would lead him to the interstate.

Chapter Thirty-Four

Elenore attempted to open her eyes, but they were far too heavy to lift. She couldn't breathe good, as if a huge weight sat on her chest.

She moaned, unable to move her arms and legs.

And then the sound of someone panting in her ear penetrated her drug-induced stupor.

It took her a moment to realize the weight on her chest belonged to a body—a body that was rapidly and roughly thrusting inside her own.

Elenore opened her mouth to scream, but nothing came out save for a weak groan.

Her eyelids cracked open enough to see a light on the ceiling above her, but her vision was too fuzzy to make out anything else.

Why couldn't she lift her arms? she wondered in a panic, unable to move her legs either.

Reality sank into her stomach like a heavy weight. She suddenly remembered fleeing the hospital and running into a stranger on the sidewalk. He'd taken her to his apartment, somewhere close by... and then drugged her.

Elenore's throat closed in horror. She'd been abused by men all her life, and there she lay, being abused once again.

Her mind snapped in that moment, and a rage unlike any she'd experienced before shot through her in a powerful rush of adrenaline.

She tried to bring her arms up once more only to realize he held them above her head.

"Easy there," he rasped, continuing his sickening trusts. "Almost done. Almost done."

Elenore gagged, bringing her legs up to kick at him with her feet.

He finally released her hands and rolled away from her. "Jesus, lady!"

The scream that had been trapped in her throat released with the power of insanity.

She rolled off the bed, landing with a *thunk* onto the floor.

Scrambling away on her knees, she continued to scream in an attempt to purge herself of the reality that was her life.

The man in the room with her landed on her back, his hand clamping painfully over her mouth. "Look, lady. I don't know what's wrong with you, but I didn't do anything to you that you didn't consent to. Do you understand?"

Elenore tried to buck him off, to no avail.

"Listen to me," he ground out against her ear. "I'm going to let you up and give you some clothes to wear. You're free to go. I'm not holding you here against your will. Got it?"

She tried to nod but found it impossible with his hand firmly against her mouth.

And then his hand left her mouth. He pushed off her back, sending relief pouring through her.

A pile of clothes abruptly landed next to her. "You can wear those."

Elenore scrambled for the items, quickly pulling the shirt over her head. With unsteady hands, she began pulling the sweatpants up over her feet.

"I don't have a car, but the hospital is only a few blocks from here. That's where you were coming from when I found you."

She tried to stand, only to fall back to the floor on her rear. "I'm not going back to the hospital. I'm going home."

"How are you going to get home? You didn't have a wallet with you when you ran into me."

"I don't know," she whispered, too disgusted by him to meet his gaze.

"Where do you live?"

Swallowing back the bile in her throat, she rasped, "Wexler."

His footsteps could be heard, slapping on the tile floor. And then his voice came from somewhere in a room to her left. It sounded as if he were calling her a cab.

With trembling hands, Elenore gathered up the cash he'd dropped next to her and stuffed it into the pocket of the sweats she wore.

She rose a little unsteadily to her feet and staggered toward the door.

"A cab will be out front to pick you up in about ten minutes," the man announced, returning to the room. "You're welcome to wait here if you want."

Elenore didn't respond. She stumbled forward, opened the door, and fell into the hall.

"Okay then." He closed the door behind her.

Pushing to her feet, Elenore zigzagged down the dimly lit corridor until she reached the exit to the street.

She practically fell outside, grabbing hold of a lamppost to stay upright.

"Hey, lady, are you okay?"

"Stay away from me!" Elenore shouted, shrinking back from the man hurrying in her direction.

He walked on past, muttering something about crazy women and drugs.

A vague memory of the evening before tickled at Elenore's conscience. The needles, unimaginable bliss. And then…nothing.

It terrified her that she'd lost bits and pieces of her memories, of her life. She wondered briefly if that was why she couldn't recall a single incident with her mother. If she'd blocked her own mother from her mind, how much more had she suppressed?

A yellow cab pulled up along the curb, jerking Elenore out of her anxious thoughts.

She stumbled forward, opened the back door, and fell inside.

The cab driver threw his arm over the back of the seat, swiveling his head in her direction. "Where to?"

"Wexler," she mumbled, turning to look out the window. "72 Haskell Road in Wexler."

The cabbie nodded, put the car in gear, and pulled out into traffic.

Elenore watched the buildings and shops fade from her view. She thought about Doctor Ingram and the nightmares he insisted she face. She thought about the baby she'd lost so long ago. She thought of her mother and wondered why she'd truly walked away. Not the stories her father had recited a dozen times in Elenore's life, but the real reason Mary Griffin had left her home and only child.

Then her mind drifted to her unborn child, a child conceived through incest or rape. Elenore wanted to shrink away from the reality of that baby growing inside her. But she couldn't.

She dragged her gaze away from that window and settled it onto her still flat abdomen. No matter how that baby had been conceived, it belonged to her, and her alone. And no matter what was in store for Elenore's future, she would never let anyone or anything hurt her child. *No one.*

Chapter Thirty-Five

Evan arrived in Albany, Georgia, trying to maneuver his car through the midmorning traffic while following the directions on his GPS.

He'd located the man Mary Griffin had run off with a little over twelve years ago.

Parking along the cul-de-sac, Evan got out and strode up the drive to the one-story, white brick house.

He rang the bell.

The door opened, and a middle-aged man appeared, holding a cat in his arms. "Morning. What can I do for you?"

Evan cleared his throat. "Ray Durden?"

"Who's asking?"

"I'm Detective Ramirez from the Haverty County Sheriff's Office in Wexler, Alabama. I was wondering if you wouldn't mind answering some questions for me?"

A shadow passed through the man's eyes, but he didn't shut the door in Evan's face. "Come on in."

Evan waited for Ray to back up a step before entering his home.

A woman with slightly graying hair sat in a recliner, knitting what appeared to be a blanket.

She greeted Evan with a smile.

"Howdy, ma'am," Evan responded with a nod.

Ray stepped up beside Evan. "Honey, this here is Detective Ramirez. He has a few questions he'd like to ask me. We'll be out in the garage."

"Is everything okay?" She paused in her knitting.

Ray sent her a reassuring look. "Everything is fine, sweetheart. I'll be back inside shortly."

"All right. There's tea in the fridge, if your guest would like a drink."

Evan shook his head. "I appreciate it, ma'am, but I'm fine."

"Ready?" Ray interjected, pulling Evan's attention back on him.

At Evan's nod, Ray strode off down a hallway.

Evan followed.

Stopping in front of a closed door, Ray turned the knob and threw it wide. "After you, Detective."

Evan stepped into the warm garage and waited for Ray to join him. "Was that your wife in there?"

"It is. What's going on?"

Clearing his throat, Evan got right to the point. "If you're married now, I take it you're no longer with Mary Griffin." It wasn't a question.

Ray Durden's eyes watered up. "Detective? Mary Griffin has been dead for nearly eight years."

That surprised Evan. "What happened?"

"Suicide."

When Evan just stood there gaping, Ray continued. "She'd been depressed for a long time. Ever since we left Wexler more than twelve years ago."

Anger reared its ugly head, but Evan held it in check. Barely. "What was her reason for leaving her daughter behind?"

The tears Ray had been fighting spilled down his cheeks. "She didn't want to leave that girl behind, Detective. She had no choice."

"Everyone has a choice, Mr. Durden."

Ray shook his head. "Not Mary. Elijah had been beating Mary since the day she said *I do*. She thought that having a child for him would change him, but it didn't. If anything, it made him worse. Then one day, she turned to me for comfort. I shouldn't have entertained the idea of having an affair with Mary. But I loved her."

"Then what happened?" Evan asked, unsympathetic to the man's plight.

"Elijah caught us together. He tried killing us both, but we managed to get away in time. When Mary went back to get her things and her daughter, Elijah told her he would kill them both and claim a murder-suicide.

"Mary tried to file charges and take him to court to get her daughter, but she was told there was nothing she could do."

"Who told her that?"

"Detective Burnham. He was tight with Elijah."

"What?" Evan asked in a deadly-soft voice. "Are you sure?"

Ray's eyes narrowed. "Oh, I'm sure, all right. I saw him myself, leaving there one night when I went over there to grab Elenore for Mary. It was around eight o'clock, and the two of them were on the porch, drinking beer."

Pieces of the puzzle began falling into place for Evan. William wasn't missing because he was investigating Elijah. He'd likely been killed to keep him quiet.

"Thank you for answering my questions, Mr. Durden. You've helped more than you know." Evan turned to go.

"Wait." Ray stood there, his arms hanging by his sides. "You never did say why you were looking for Mary."

Evan debated on how much to tell him. He looked at the man with his red-rimmed eyes and hedged. "I've taken over at the sheriff's department as the new detective, and I'm investigating Elijah Griffin. I thought, or hoped rather, that Mary might be able to shed some light on where Griffin might be. Have a good day, Mr. Durden."

Evan moved toward the side door of the garage. He stopped in front of it with his hand on the knob and looked back over his shoulder. "Can you tell me where Mary is buried?"

Ray nodded. "At the Oakwood Cemetery on 19th Street."

Opening the door, Evan stepped outside and strode to his car. He would visit Mary's grave and eventually bring Elenore there…for closure.

Chapter Thirty-Six

Evan arrived back in Wexler a little after four o'clock that afternoon. He'd visited Mary Griffin's grave, surprised to see a nice headstone resting there. Ray Durden must have really loved her.

Parking out front, Evan exited his vehicle and entered the station in search of the sheriff.

Tom looked up from his dispatch cubicle. "Hey, Detective."

Evan slowed his steps. "Is Sheriff King around?"

"No, sir. He's at a function with the mayor, but he should be back soon. Is there something I can do to help?"

Evan shook his head. "Thanks, Tom, but I'll just wait on the sheriff. I'll be in my office, looking over some casework. Will you let him know I need to see him?"

"Sure thing, Detective."

Making his way to the back where his office was situated, Evan dropped heavily into his chair.

He opened the file in front of him and stared blankly at the words.

With a heavy sigh, he shoved the folder away and leaned his head back on his shoulders. *Where are you, Elenore?*

Long moments passed with Evan going over every scenario he could conjure up. Everything from where Elenore could possibly be, to which ditch she might be lying in.

He surged to his feet and turned to stare out the window at the street beyond. Elenore was out there somewhere, pregnant and likely terrified. She had no money or friends to turn to.

"You wanted to see me?"

Evan turned to find the sheriff standing in the open doorway. "Yes, sir. Would you mind coming inside and closing the door?"

Donnie's eyebrows lifted. He stepped forward, pushing the door shut behind him. "Sounds serious."

"It is." Taking a deep breath, Evan launched into the story of his trip to Birmingham, ending with, "Burnham is involved in all this."

The sheriff's face turned red with anger. "William was a very good investigator, Detective. Just because someone thinks they saw him drinking a beer with Griffin doesn't make him the bad guy here. Knowing William, he was there trying to win the man's trust."

A muscle ticked along Evan's jaw. "I'd like to go back out there and look again. Maybe we missed something. And did we ever get anything back on the fireplace poker?"

The sheriff lifted a hand. "Slow down. The blood on the fireplace poker belonged to Elenore, and Elenore alone. As for going back out there, are you referring to the Griffin place?"

Evan held the sheriff's gaze and crossed his arms over his chest. "I am."

"You can't go back, Detective. That warrant was a one-time gig. It expired the second we left that place after the initial search. And you can believe that the new judge isn't going to issue another one. We have no probable cause."

Evan had to unclench his teeth in order to respond. "So, what now? We just sit idly by and let Griffin get away with murder?"

The sheriff momentarily closed his eyes as if praying for patience. "You keep digging until you find something we can work with, Detective. Until then, stay away from the Griffin place. Do I make myself clear?"

"Perfectly," Evan bit out, holding Donnie's gaze. "In the meantime, you should know that Mary Griffin is dead."

That gave the sheriff pause. "What happened to her?"

"Suicide, a few years back. I guess she couldn't deal with the repercussions of leaving her daughter with that monster."

Sadness appeared in Donnie's eyes. "I'm truly sorry to hear that, Detective. No matter what you might think, I do care about what happens in my town. But we *will* go by the book with Griffin. When he's caught, and he will be caught, I want him nailed to the cross. Not walking away a free man because we didn't do our jobs right."

Evan sighed. "I know. It just ticks me off that poor Elenore has had to live with that monster all her life, and no one could help her. As for Judge Powell, wherever he is, I hope he got what he deserved. And the rest of the men missing from town, I have a feeling they were just as involved with Griffin as Powell was."

"That may be true, Detective, but until we have proof of that, we stick to the book, and we do our job."

"Okay, so we can't search the premises again, but that doesn't mean we can't stake out the place and wait for him to return."

Donnie's face reddened once more. "We don't have the manpower to stake out the Griffin place. I have four deputies assigned to Wexler. Four, Detective. Do your job. Talk to witnesses and find evidence that Griffin killed those men. Then come talk to me."

Evan remained standing long after the sheriff departed. He wouldn't be able to search Elijah Griffin's place again.

Rage boiled up inside him. How were they expected to find him, sitting around with their thumbs up their butts?

Well, orders could get screwed. Evan had no intentions of sitting behind a desk, sifting through papers, while that demon walked free.

He snatched up his keys and left the station.

Chapter Thirty-Seven

Evan arrived at his apartment less than five minutes after leaving the station.

He hurried inside, stripping out of his uniform on his way to the bedroom.

Opening a drawer, he pulled a black T-shirt free, along with a pair of jeans.

Evan dressed in record time, tugging on a pair of running shoes and checking his watch. He had about thirty minutes before dark would fall—thirty minutes until he could head to Elijah's.

Pacing his small living room, Evan thought about everything he'd learned so far. Elijah Griffin had used Alice Hastings, a local prostitute, to sell his daughter to Judge Powell. Truth be told, Griffin had probably sold Elenore to Alan Brown, Dennis Baker, and Hector Gonzalez as well.

Of course, Evan had no proof to back that up. But his gut had been screaming it since he'd visited Wanda, Alan Brown's wife.

William Burnham was definitely involved. Not only had Ray Durden witnessed him drinking with Griffin, but Evan had found that photo of Alice in the top of Burnham's closet.

Once he'd finished preparing, Evan left his apartment and climbed behind the wheel of his personal car. His patrol could be tracked. As could his cell phone, which was why he'd left it on his kitchen table.

He drove the speed limit out of town until he came to the dirt road that led to the Griffin farm.

Evan's palms grew sweaty, forcing him to scrub them along his jeans to keep them from sliding on the steering wheel.

The Griffin farm lay just ahead.

He noticed a light on in the barn as he drove past. Of course, Charlie could have left it on after feeding the animals.

Making sure no other cars were coming up the dirt road, Evan parked along the side and quietly climbed out.

He crept through the woods in order to come up on the left side of the house. No lights were on inside, nor were there any vehicles in the drive.

Evan silently moved to the porch and tried the knob. It opened easily.

He eased through the living room and took a left toward Elijah's room. The sheriff had searched that room, and honestly, Evan wasn't sure how much he trusted the guy. Donnie had been way too quick to defend William Burnham.

More anger surfaced. Was the sheriff involved with Griffin as well? Evan was beginning to wonder.

Pulling the small flashlight from the pocket of his jeans, Evan set about searching Elijah's domain.

He tugged open drawers, looked through the nightstand, and thoroughly searched the closet. But there was nothing anywhere that implicated the man in the disappearances of Brown, Gonzalez, or Baker. There was also no evidence on Judge Powell or William Burnham.

Evan looked through the rest of the house but came up empty there as well. Whatever Elijah was involved in, he'd efficiently covered his tracks.

Feeling more than a little defeated, Evan trailed through the kitchen and exited the back door.

He might as well turn off the barn light while he was there. The animals probably wouldn't sleep with it on.

The stall door where the milk cow resided stood ajar. Evan unsnapped the holster where his 9mm rested and tugged it free.

He inched silently forward, his heartbeat thumping in his ears.

Evan swung around, weapon at the ready, but there was no one in the stall but the cow.

He continued on, checking the rest of the stalls but they were all clear. He holstered his weapon and headed back toward the main entrance.

Stopping along the way to latch the stall door, Evan reached inside and rubbed the top of the cow's head. "Hey there, girl."

He was about to turn and leave when something protruding through the hay caught his eye.

"What is that?"

Opening the short wooden door, Evan shooed the cow out of the stall and stepped inside.

He moved to the stall's center and dropped to his haunches. There, hidden beneath the hay, was an iron latch of some kind.

Evan brushed aside the hay to reveal a wooden hatch approximately four feet wide by four feet long.

He quickly glanced around, his heart beating in his throat, and then carefully lifted the hatch.

An overwhelmingly foul odor blasted Evan in the face, telling him without words that he'd found the missing men from Wexler.

Torn between closing that door and waiting for a warrant or following his gut and going in, Evan chose the latter.

He tugged the flashlight free of his jeans once more and shined the light into the hole.

The smell that wafted up to greet him was almost more than Evan could take.

He lifted the collar of his T-shirt, pulled it over his nose, and moved the light around the hole. Only it wasn't simply a hole. It was a large room carved from dirt.

Listening to be sure that he was alone, Evan twisted his body around and rested his foot on a ladder leading below.

Once near the bottom, he released his hold on the ladder and dropped the few feet to the ground.

Evan moved his flashlight in a wide arc until he found what he looked for. A lantern set along the wall on a wooden shelf, with a small box of matches perched next to it.

Laying the flashlight on the shelf, Evan struck a match and lit the lantern, then lifted it high above his head.

A small box could be seen nestled in the corner of the shelf. Evan tugged it toward him and held the lantern above it.

Inside were several wallets, a few watches, and some rings.

He set the lantern on the shelf next to him and fished out the first wallet. Inside was the license of Hector Gonzalez.

Laying that one aside, he plucked up the next one, only to discover the mug of Dennis Baker smiling back at him. The next wallet belonged to Alan Brown and the next to Judge Powell.

Two more wallets remained.

Attempting to breathe through the putrid smell surrounding him, Evan opened the next wallet. It, of course, belonged to William Burnham, just as Evan thought it would.

Evan stared into that box for a moment longer before tugging the last wallet free.

Flipping it open, Evan blinked in disbelief at the license of Elijah Griffin.

It couldn't be, but the evidence of it stared back at him in the form of the sadistic monster who'd abused his daughter all her life.

Replacing the wallets back in the box, Evan snatched up the lantern and eased across the dirt room to a pile of blankets and tarps along the wall.

He bent low, grabbed the corner of a blanket, and peeled it back.

Elijah's milky-colored eyes stared blankly up at him.

Evan gagged, recovering his nose with his T-shirt.

His mind began to race with the implication of finding Elijah dead.

The sheriff's narrowed eyes suddenly flashed through Evan's mind. He recalled the day they'd searched the house, how the sheriff had reacted to Evan finding that fireplace poker. How he'd ordered Evan not to return to the Griffin farm. How he'd insisted that Charlie feed Elenore's animals instead of Evan.

Lifting the lantern higher, Evan pulled at another blanket and another, each time uncovering another half-rotted body until he'd found the remains of every person matching the wallets in that box.

He needed to get out of there and figure out what to do. If the sheriff found him there, he would no doubt bury Evan right alongside the others.

Evan was just about to leave when an old, dusty tarp in the corner caught his eye.

He moved in closer, tugging the tarp free. "What in God's name?"

The skeleton of a woman sat propped up in the corner, an old, ragged baby doll in her arms.

Strands of dark hair protruded from the skeleton's head, and a yellow purse hung over her bony shoulder.

What was left of a short jean skirt and a tank top were still attached to the dead woman's body.

Evan leaned in close and opened the purse, careful not to disturb the scene. Inside was a small feminine wallet. He tugged it free and shined the light on the license inside.

"Alice Hastings," Evan murmured, glancing back at the woman's skeleton. "Looks like you got exactly what you deserved."

"They all did," a voice rasped from behind him. "Every last one of them."

Evan dropped the purse he held, unable to believe what he'd just heard.

He slowly turned around to find a 9mm aimed at his chest.

Too stunned to move, Evan whispered, "Elenore?"

She pulled the trigger.

"I am Elle…"

Don't miss Elle Returns, book two in the Elle series. Available on Amazon!

Read below for a sneak peek into the pages of The Silencer: A Gripping Thriller

Chapter One

Oliver Quick rubbed at his bloodshot eyes and glanced at the blinking phone on his desk.

He wondered how long the caller would hold before growing impatient and hanging up altogether.

The door to his office abruptly opened and his secretary, Joyce Meeks, poked her head inside.

She stared at him with a disapproving look before marching across the room to snatch up the phone. "I apologize for the wait, Mr. Williams. Oliver is on another line. I'd be happy to take a message if you'd rather not continue to hold."

Oliver listened to Joyce repeat his brother-in-law, Aaron Williams's, words back to him, understanding full well she did it for his own benefit.

Joyce Meeks had been with Oliver since he'd opened Quick Investigations a little more than five years ago. Though she spoke with the voice of a seasoned general and wore her hair in a similar fashion, she had kind blue eyes. And she thought of Oliver as the son she never had.

She returned the phone receiver to its home with a little more force than was probably necessary and pierced Oliver with an accessing stare. "Too much scotch last night?"

Oliver leaned back in his chair, propping his feet on the corner of his desk, and ignored Joyce's reference to his late-night drinking. "What did Aaron want?"

"Besides calling to invite you to the children's birthday party next weekend? I have no idea. Why don't you call him back and find out?"

Oliver inwardly cringed. Spending his weekend with a bunch of screaming kids didn't bode well with his hangover.

He opened his mouth to announce that very thing, when the trill of the phone once again echoed from his desk, sending an unwelcome pain shooting through his skull.

"Serves you right," Joyce snapped, striding toward the open door. "That drinking is going to be the death of you." The door clicked shut behind her.

"Quick Investigations," Oliver nearly growled, answering the incoming call.

A brief pause ensued. "Hello, Oliver, it's Richard Holland."

Oliver's stomach tightened. There would be only one reason the supervisor of the FBI field office in Huntsville, Alabama would be calling him. They needed his help.

"SSA Holland," Quick acknowledged. "It's been a minute." *Nearly six years to be exact.*

Richard cleared his throat. "That it has. Look, Quick, I could use your help."

"My help? With what?" But Oliver knew. He'd already heard about the dismembered body discovered under the pier in Panama City Beach. It was all over the news. "I'm not a profiler any longer, Richard. I haven't been for years."

"A profiler isn't something you do, Quick. It's who you are."

Oliver refrained from pointing out the obvious. The last serial killer he'd profiled had not only killed Oliver's wife, he'd gone on to kill six more women shortly afterward.

"I'm headed to Panama City Beach," Richard continued without preamble. "Can you meet me for lunch?"

The last thing Oliver needed was the smell of greasy food invading his hungover, consistently throbbing head. But the profiler in him couldn't resist meeting with the leader of the Behavioral Analysis Unit in Huntsville. "Salty Sue's in half an hour."

"I'll be there." The line went dead.

Oliver replaced the phone receiver and stood. He wandered over to his large office window to stare out at the busy Destin traffic of Back Beach Road.

His hands sank into the pockets of his navy-blue slacks. He watched the cars move bumper-to-bumper in an impatient line of horn-blowing maniacs.

April had loved this place, Oliver thought, his gaze moving to the beach beyond. She'd wanted to raise their children there…children they would never have.

The old, familiar ache that always began in his heart with thoughts of April traveled through his chest to settle in his gut.

Nausea was instant.

Oliver locked his teeth together, his eyes sliding closed to shut out the view before him.

He groaned deep in his throat, allowing the memories of his beautiful April to wash through him.

Her laughter, the always present twinkle in her pretty green eyes, and the dimple in her cheek when she smiled flashed behind his closed lids with haunting clarity.

His mind instantly rebelled against what he knew would come next, but he could no longer block it out than he could stop the waves from crashing onto the shore of the beach in front of him.

April lying in that morgue. A perfectly straight incision on her bruised and battered throat. Her larynx had been removed with the precision of a surgeon and then the wound sewn closed.

Oliver shuddered, unable to push the images from his mind. His wife, his precious April had been repeatedly raped, violated in the vilest of ways. Her breasts had been burned in numerous places, along with her genitals.

She'd been bound for days, unable to speak or scream while her killer endlessly tortured her to death. He'd then painted her fingernails and toenails a blood-red color…postmortem.

April had been his sixth victim in less than a month, categorizing him as a serial killer. He'd been dubbed *the Silencer* by the media for removing his victim's voice boxes days before he ended their lives. And then he'd painted their fingernails and toenails. Always with the same red color.

"Oliver?"

Somewhere in the far recesses of his mind, Oliver knew Joyce spoke to him, but he couldn't seem to pull back from the grief swimming inside him. He hadn't caught April's killer. His profile had been off.

The Silencer had vanished almost six years ago, leaving no evidence to his identity behind.

Oliver had worked day and night to profile the sicko, only to come up empty. He'd been too close to the case, making him less than objective.

His emotions, grief and helpless rage over the loss of his wife, had stood between him and his ability to be open-minded and detached.

The Silencer had slipped through his fingers.

A hand rested against Quick's back, and his secretary's voice finally penetrated his guilt-filled mind. "Oliver, are you all right?"

He swallowed with more than a little difficulty. "I'm fine, Joyce. Thank you."

"There's a man here to see you."

He answered without turning away from the window. "Have him make an appointment. I'm meeting someone in ten minutes for lunch."

"But—"

"Please, Joyce. I can't do this right now."

Something in his voice must have clued her in to his current mental status. Her hand fell away, and the sound of her shoes slapping on the tile floor could be heard over the horns blowing from the streets beyond.

Oliver waited until the door closed behind her, then trailed to his desk, plucked up his suit jacket, and left by way of the back.

Chapter Two

Richard Holland waited until the waitress moved away before extending his hand across the table to Oliver. "Thank you for coming on such short notice."

Oliver accepted the man's outstretched palm and took a seat. "It's good to see you, Richard. So, tell me what you've got."

Holland nodded, pushing a yellow folder toward Oliver. "You always did get right to the point."

Opening the folder, Oliver took in the sight before him.

Dozens of photos were inside; images of the dismembered body of the female found beneath the pier in Panama City Beach.

Oliver hardened himself against his emotions. "I understand the heinousness of the crime, but why has the FBI been called in on this?"

Richard set his water glass down and wiped his mouth with a cloth napkin. "Because there were two similar cases last month less than an hour from here over the Alabama line. The Baldwin County Sheriff's Office called us in to assist."

Oliver's jaw tightened. "Similar cases?"

"There's enough similarities for us to ascertain it's the same guy."

"A serial killer," Oliver stated in a deadly-soft tone.

Richard nodded. "The Bay County Police Department notified us of the body found beneath the pier. They called in the local sheriff's department and the FBI to help with the investigation. My team is there now."

April's cold, pale body flashed behind Oliver's eyes. "Why are you coming to me with this? You have an efficient team working with you in Huntsville and a dozen more at your disposal at the Quantico office."

"Because you're one of the best profilers I've ever known, and I'd like your help with this."

Oliver closed the folder and got to his feet. "I'm a private investigator now. I no longer hunt serial killers, Richard. I haven't since—"

"Since April died," Richard interrupted, catching Oliver off guard.

"I understand your reluctance, Quick." Richard leaned across the table and flipped the folder back open. "But this woman had a family, a husband...and a child on the way. She can't tell us who did this to her, but I'm willing to bet that you can."

Richard lifted a picture of the woman's decapitated head and held it up for Oliver to see. "Her husband needs closure. As do her parents."

Oliver stared down into the lifeless eyes of the woman in the picture for long moments. She'd been pregnant…just as April had.

Swallowing back the bile that rose in his throat, Oliver tore his gaze from the sickening photo and returned to his seat.

As badly as he wanted to, he simply couldn't bring himself to walk away. "What's the victim's name?"

"Clayton. Jennifer Clayton."

Oliver let that sink in. "I'll need to see the scene where the body was found."

Richard placed the picture back in the folder and tucked it inside his briefcase. "I'll take you there right after you get some food in you. From the look of your eyes, you could use it."

Oliver wasn't hungry, but he would order anyway. He needed something to soak up the overabundance of alcohol from the night before. And he needed strength for what he knew lay ahead.

* * * *

After driving to his condo to change into jeans and running shoes, Oliver donned his Oakley's and followed Holland to the normally busy beach in Panama City.

The expected yellow tape and police presence surrounded the massive pier to keep onlookers from contaminating what was left of the crime scene.

The rising tide from the previous two nights had no doubt destroyed what evidence had been left behind. Which Oliver doubted would be any.

But it wasn't evidence Oliver looked for. Most serial killers were meticulous. They didn't leave behind incriminating evidence. No, he needed to see what the killer saw, hear what he heard…and figure out why he chose that particular place to dispose of the body.

Oliver trailed along behind Holland, his gaze touching on everything around him. From the mobs of curious onlookers to the surrounding storefronts and restaurants in close proximity to the pier.

His gaze then swung to the dunes behind him, coming to rest on the taped-off markings embedded in the sand. *Drag marks, most likely from a body.*

How had the killer dragged a bag of body parts down to the pier without being noticed by anyone?

The crowd of people gathered around, attempted to move in closer, forcing the police to order them back.

Though it had been two days since Jennifer Clayton's body had been discovered, the onlookers hadn't seemed to grow bored with the taped-off crime scene.

As if reading Oliver's thoughts, Richard stepped in closer to his side. "It's going to be like this for a while longer, I'm sure. With so much sand and the size of that pier, God knows how long it'll take them to finish processing the scene."

A middle-aged officer keeping the crowds back turned as Holland and Oliver approached the tape.

Holland produced his credentials, spoke a few words to the officer while jerking his chin in Oliver's direction.

Oliver nodded to the officer, ducking beneath the yellow tape the officer lifted for him and then held up a hand, indicating he wanted to go down alone.

Holland didn't attempt to follow, nor did Oliver expect him to. He'd worked with the man long enough in the past to know that Richard understood his particular profiling methods.

Oliver didn't bother to search the sugary white beach sand around the pier. He wouldn't find anything there. Besides, the local police department was still crawling through the scene with the precision of ants erecting a mound.

With so much sand in the vicinity, they were forced to sift through it, inch by inch.

Shutting out everything around him, Oliver's mind slipped into profiler mode. His vision grew tunneled and his senses became heightened. Sounds from the crashing waves of the Gulf faded to the background, along with the murmuring of voices surrounding the crime scene.

The bright noonday sun turned into a silvery moon in Oliver's mind, casting shadows along the dunes and sending the long, giant pier plummeting into darkness.

Oliver's head swiveled to the right as he imagined the lights along the rails of the pier coming on at sunset.

His gaze traveled to the local restaurant sitting a short distance up the beach. Music spilled out from the open deck to be swept away on the warm moonlit breeze.

The lights shone brightly through the fog hovering over the Gulf, illuminating the dunes between the deck of the restaurant and the pier.

Smiling faces of tourists moved through his mind, their laughter and friendly banter growing in volume in order to be heard over the music thumping in the background.

No one from that deck would likely notice a lone figure making their way beneath the pier.

His gaze swept to the left, to a souvenir shop that probably closed their doors at five o'clock sharp on the weekdays. No danger of being seen from there.

On it went, with Oliver studying his surroundings, an imaginary garbage bag in his hand growing heavier with each passing second.

He imaged himself pulling in to the parking lot up the hill, waiting for his opportunity to move.

But why the busy pier area? There are literally hundreds of miles of beachfront to dump a body. Yet he chose this particular spot. Why…?

Because he's a narcissist. Torture isn't enough for him. He garners some kind of rush from the threat of exposure. He believes the women are beneath him. He thinks himself superior…

The face of the decapitated woman appeared in Oliver's mind, pulling him back from the abyss, back to the dozens of eyes watching him expectantly.

He sought out Holland, who promptly moved to his side.

"What are you thinking, Quick?"

Oliver held the shorter man's gaze. "I'd need to see the autopsy results to be sure, but I'm willing to bet that the unsub drowned the victim before cutting her up."

"What makes you think that?"

Oliver shrugged. "He's grandstanding by bringing her out here and leaving her to be found. But the water, the water is significant to him somehow."

"Then why cut her up?"

"I don't know yet," Oliver stated in a matter-of-fact tone. "But I'd like to see the body now."

"Okay. Let's go."

Oliver strode along next to Holland, his mind still mulling over the surrounding establishments. "Are there any cameras on the restaurant and souvenir shop?"

Richard shook his head. "Some of the shops down the beach have cameras, but the ones closest to the pier don't."

"I'm betting he knew that," Oliver admitted with near certainty. "He's been in both places. More than once."

Holland's gaze narrowed. "He cased the places before he chose this spot."

"Exactly."

They reached the parking area at the top of the hill. Holland hesitated before opening his car door. "I'll have the receipts pulled at both places for the last month. Hopefully we get a hit on something."

Oliver nodded, fishing his keys out of the pocket of his jeans. "I'd like to question the staff myself. Once I've seen the body."

Richard slid behind the wheel of his vehicle. "Follow me."

Chapter Three

Oliver arrived at the medical examiner's office behind Holland twenty minutes later.

The two men entered the building, side by side, making their way to the back where the refrigerated bodies were held.

It had been years since Oliver had darkened the door of the place.

Not much had changed, he noted, recognizing the familiar scent of the chemicals used in the back. It was a smell he would know anywhere. A smell he associated with…death.

A pretty brunette exited the lady's room on the left, nearly running into Quick in the process.

She barely flinched. "Excuse me, gentlemen, may I help you?"

Oliver pushed his Oakley's to the top of his head.

He swiftly took in her appearance, noting her air of confidence and the direct look she gave him without breaking eye contact.

She was no doubt used to dealing with his type. And by his type, he meant suits. Even though he wore jeans at the moment.

Richard produced his credentials. "We're with the FBI. We need to see the body of the dismembered female that was recently brought in."

The brunette eyed his identification. "I'm assuming you've been here before and know your way around."

"We have," Richard assured her, returning his ID to his pocket.

She simply nodded before skirting them both, the clicking of her heels echoing off the hallway walls as she strode away.

Richard ambled ahead, stopping outside the door that read, *Medical Examiner*.

He rapped on it once with his knuckles and then turned the knob, entering the chilled room without further notice.

Oliver trailed in behind him, blocking out the smells invading his senses.

A man Oliver hadn't met before stood over a stainless-steel table, the florescent lights above him reflecting off his partially bald head. His gloved hands hovered above the corpse of a man that appeared to be in his late fifties.

The tag on the doctor's coat pocket read, *Dr. T. Ramsey.*

Ramsey peered up over the rim of his glasses, glancing at Oliver and then Richard. "Holland. I figured you'd be down here before long."

"Hello, Evan," Holland greeted, approaching the table. "Have you met my associate, Oliver Quick?"

The doctor shook his head, meeting Oliver's gaze. "I haven't had the pleasure, but I've certainly heard of you. Your reputation as a profiler is remarkable."

Oliver brushed the compliment aside, uncomfortable with the praise. As was his way, he got right to the point. "Has Jennifer Clayton's body been autopsied?"

Ramsey sent him a quick nod. "It has. She was top priority." He jerked his chin toward the refrigerated drawers along the opposite wall. "She's in number eighteen."

"Thank you, Doctor." Oliver trailed across the room, pulling open the designated drawer.

The chilly air of the refrigeration sent goosebumps peppering his arms.

He stared down at the black body bag, remembering back to when he'd had to identify April.

His heart began to pound, dread and nausea growing stronger by the second.

"Is everything all right?"

The sound of Richard's voice broke into his anxiety.

With a surprisingly steady hand, Oliver took hold of the body bag's zipper and slowly glided it down. He stopped when Jennifer's head came into view.

The sight of a corpse always unsettled him. But the murdered ones… The murdered ones were the worst. The frozen terror in their eyes, as if they took those last horrendous moments with them to eternity.

Doctor Ramsey appeared on the opposite side of the drawer, holding a folder in his hands.

Oliver raised his gaze to the doctor's. "What was the cause of death?"

"Drowning. Repeatedly."

Surely Oliver hadn't heard him right. "I'm sorry, did you say repeatedly?"

Ramsey opened the folder and pulled a paper free. He handed it to Oliver. "Those were my findings. She'd been drowned more than once, resuscitated only to be drowned again. It's hard to tell the exact number of times this was done to her. I can only assure you that it's what killed her."

Oliver glanced down into the woman's milky-colored eyes and then met the doctor's gaze once more. "So, he cut the body up postmortem." It wasn't a question.

"Most of the body," the doctor muttered, unzipping the bag the rest of the way. He reached inside and lifted a pale-colored hand up for Oliver's perusal. The ring finger was missing. "The fourth finger was removed before her death, as was the fetus she carried."

Oliver digested that bit of information, swallowing back the bile that rose in his throat. Jennifer Clayton's unborn child had been removed from her body before her death.

Unclenching his teeth enough to speak, Oliver asked, "Was the baby vaginally removed or…"

The doctor shook his head. "He was cut from the abdomen and then the wound sewn closed."

"He…" Oliver began.

"The gender of the fetus was discovered from the victim's medical records," Dr. Ramsey offered, saving Oliver the task of asking the dreaded question aloud.

Getting a grip on his emotions, Oliver shut them down completely. "I take it the fetus wasn't recovered?"

"No, I'm afraid not," Ramsey answered.

Oliver let that sink in. "How far along was Mrs. Clayton in her pregnancy?"

Doctor Ramsey's gaze softened. "Thirty-two weeks."

Oliver briefly glanced at Holland. "That's four deaths he's responsible for. Not three."

Without waiting for a response from Richard, Oliver nailed the doctor with another question. "Was a wedding ring recovered?"

Richard answered for the doctor. "Nothing has been recovered. Not her clothes, jewelry, or her car."

Pinching the bridge of his nose, Oliver questioned the doctor further. "Was there any evidence of rape, strangulation, any ligature marks or other wounds besides the obvious?"

The doctor nodded. "There were ligature marks on her wrists, consistent with rope. We also found some marks and residue on her lower face, telling us that her mouth had been duct taped for quite some time. I found no evidence of rape."

That surprised Oliver. According to Richard, both the women discovered in Alabama had been raped. "How long was Mrs. Clayton missing before her body was found?"

"A week," Richard answered quietly.

Oliver's detachment momentarily slipped. Jennifer Clayton had been tortured, drowned, and resuscitated, only to be tortured again and again before the killer grew tired and drowned her a final time. But not before he cut her unborn child from her body.

"He tortured her for a week." Oliver took a step back and met Holland's gaze. "That's almost unheard of, Richard. Most serial killers don't last beyond three days before their rage drives them to kill."

When Holland simply stood there, silently watching him, Oliver asked, "Was the MO the same with the Alabama victims?"

Richard nodded his confirmation. "Aside from the fact they'd been raped, both victims were found along the shore of the Gulf in Alabama, their dismembered bodies stuffed into garbage bags and tied to a dock."

Oliver knew the answer to his next question, but he asked it anyway. "Private or public docks?"

"Public. Why?"

"It's the epilogue to his fantasy." Oliver glanced between Holland and Ramsey. "His last show of humiliation before he moves beyond them in search of a new vic."

A deep indention appeared between Ramsey's eyes. "And the finger he removes?"

Oliver returned his attention to the woman's hand, the doctor still held. "Since it's customary to wear a wedding ring on that particular finger, my guess is it's significant to him somehow. A cheating wife or girlfriend."

Ramsey placed the hand back inside the body bag and zipped it up. "Are you saying he removes the finger as a form of punishment?"

Oliver shrugged. "Partly. But it's definitely his signature. And he's most likely keeping the wedding rings as trophies."

"But why the babies?" Richard asked. "Why take pregnant women?"

Oliver swung his gaze in Richard's direction. "Were the other fetuses removed in the same manner as Jennifer Clayton's?"

Richard slightly shook his head. "According to the reports, the unborn children hadn't been removed."

"Then why was Jennifer's?" Oliver peered down at the now zipped bag containing

Jennifer's body, watching as Dr. Ramsey slowly eased her drawer back into its refrigeration unit.

Oliver spun on his heel and headed toward the door without a word to either of the men behind him.

"Quick?" Richard caught up with Oliver as he stepped into the hall. "What are you thinking?"

Oliver didn't slow. "I need to see the reports from the two vics in Alabama."

"I can get them to you within the hour, but you haven't answered my question."

Sailing out the double doors to the parking lot beyond, Oliver dug out his car keys and paused next to his vehicle. "The killer saw something in Jennifer Clayton, something he didn't see in the others."

Oliver unlocked his door and pulled it open. "He removed her unborn child from her body."

"Plus, Jennifer Clayton hadn't been raped," Richard unnecessarily pointed out."

"Yeah," Oliver muttered softly, more to himself than for Richard's benefit. "And I need to know what changed for him with Jennifer. Something changed." With that, he slid behind the wheel, cranked the stifling hot SUV, and backed out of the parking lot.

Chapter Four

Oliver sat on his couch later that evening, drink and folder in hand. He couldn't get Jennifer Clayton out of his mind.

She'd had her unborn child removed from her body before her death. *Why?*

Mrs. Clayton had been a twenty-eight-year-old preschool teacher with her whole life ahead of her…her hopes and dreams snuffed out by a sadistic monster bent on pain and humiliation.

Opening the folder, Oliver scanned the details of the first page until he found what he looked for… Jennifer's husband, Mark Clayton.

Mark was a sales rep for a local pest control company in town. He was thirty-two years old, just four years older than his deceased wife.

Oliver made a mental note to visit Mr. Clayton first thing the following morning.

He laid the folder aside and picked up the next one. Inside were images and details of one of the women found in Alabama. Blonde hair, blue eyes, twenty-seven years of age.

Laying that folder aside, Oliver opened the next one only to find similarities to the other two victims. Same hair and eye color.

He glanced at the woman's age, not surprised to find she'd been under thirty at the time of her death as well.

The victims aren't random. They're surrogates.

Oliver took another swig of his scotch, glancing at the clock on the wall. It was closing in on ten pm.

He set his drink on the coffee table, along with the folders he held, and then snatched up his cell phone and put in a call to his secretary, Joyce.

She answered on the third ring. "Hello?"

"Hi, Joyce. I'm not going to be in the office the rest of the week. Will you call my sister and let her know that I won't be making the birthday party tomorrow?"

"Is everything all right?" Though she sounded sleepy, concern lined the edges of her voice.

Oliver chose his words carefully. "Everything is fine, Joyce. I've been asked to profile for the BAU on a local case."

"The BAU? I thought you were done working with them."

"It's only temporary, I promise. I'd like for you to keep the office open in my absence."

His secretary remained quiet for a moment. "It's obviously something serious if they need a profiler. Should I be concerned?"

Since she wasn't a young blonde, Oliver knew she had nothing to worry about.

He attempted to put her mind at ease. "Not at all, Joyce. Hopefully, we'll have everything wrapped up quickly, and I'll be back in the office before you know it."

A brief pause ensued. "Okay. I'll call Mindy and let her know you can't make the party. If you need my help with anything, just let me know."

"Thank you, Joyce. Just knowing you're taking care of the office is more help than anything. Have a good night."

He hung up the phone and placed it on the coffee table next to the folders before downing the rest of his scotch.

The doorbell rang, eliciting an annoyed growl in the back of his throat.

He surged to his feet and marched across the room.

A look through the peephole conjured up Jason Haney's face.

Oliver opened the door and stepped back to allow his lifelong friend's entrance. "You're out kind of late."

Jason sauntered into the room and made his way to the bar to pour himself a drink. "It's only ten fifteen. Can I get you a refill?"

Oliver handed him his empty glass and followed him to the bar.

"What are you up to this evening?" Jason quickly poured them two drinks.

Oliver waited for Jason to pass him his scotch and then took a deep swallow. "I'm actually working."

"At this hour?"

Oliver rubbed at the back of his neck. "I've been asked to assist the FBI on a case."

With his glass to his lips, Jason turned to face Oliver, his eyebrows nearly in his hairline. "No kidding?"

Oliver returned to his position on the couch and waited for Jason to take a seat across from him in the recliner. "I was a bit surprised, myself. I mean it's been years."

Jason sat forward with his elbows resting on his jean-clad knees, swirling the dark liquid around in his scotch glass. "You're profiling again?"

Oliver shrugged. "Not on a permanent basis. I'm merely assisting them on a local case."

Understanding registered in Jason's brown eyes. "Ah. The girl that was found under the pier in Panama City Beach."

"Yes," Oliver admitted before taking a drink of his scotch. "Two more were killed earlier in the month over the Alabama line. Same MO."

Jason stared back at him without blinking. "A serial killer. Are you going to be able to handle this?"

Oliver understood Jason's concern. He'd watched Oliver fall apart after April's death and had been by his side through the frustration and rage of letting her killer slip through his fingers. "I can handle it."

But he wasn't so sure he believed his own words.

Jason continued to stare, his dark brown eyes brimming with concern.

"I said I can handle it," Oliver bit out, more annoyed with himself than with Jason.

"Okay then." Jason sighed. "I'll let it drop. Just know that I'm here if you need to talk." He finished off his drink, set the empty glass on the coffee table, and pushed to his feet. "I have to go. I'm meeting someone at Gulfscape in half an hour."

Oliver stood as well. "You have a date at eleven o'clock?"

Jason grinned. "Jealous?"

"Not at all. I'm perfectly content sleeping alone. But you go and have a good time. I'll just live vicariously through you."

Jason sobered. "It's been almost six years, Quick. Don't you think it's about time you lived a little?"

Oliver knew his friend spoke the truth, but he couldn't bring himself to enter the dating scene. Not yet. "I'm far too screwed up to attempt dating. My emotional baggage alone is enough to outweigh the best of intentions."

With an understanding nod, Jason made his way to the door and pulled it open. He stopped on the porch of Oliver's beachside condo, appearing to consider his next words. "We all miss her, my friend. She was a heck of a lady. A lady that would want you to go on living. Even if it means without her."

Jason trailed off the porch and sauntered over to his Harley parked next to Oliver's black SUV.

He plucked up his helmet and threw his leg over the bike. "Think about what I said."

Oliver merely nodded. "Since when did you start wearing a helmet?"

"Since I let my insurance lapse. You know how Florida laws are. If you don't carry insurance, you have to cover the bean."

Oliver grinned, watching Jason pull the helmet over his shaggy blond hair.

"Give it hell," Oliver called out before closing the door. He blew out an exhausted breath, grabbed up the empty glasses, and carried them to the sink at the bar.

Memories of April's smiling face bombarded him as he grabbed a sponge, turned on the water, and absently began to wash out the glass he held.

"You really should get the black leather sofa, Oliver. It suits your sexy, profiling self."

Her husky laughter swirled through his mind, bringing with it nearly unbearable pain.

The sound of glass shattering brought Oliver out of his musings. He'd been so caught up in his memories, he hadn't realized how much pressure he'd applied to the glass.

He dropped the sponge, his gaze now fixated on the steady stream of blood washing down the drain.

He'd cut his hand.

Deep.

Snatching up a dish towel, he wrapped it tightly around the now throbbing wound and grabbed his keys from the counter on his way to the door.

Available on Amazon

Titles by Ditter Kellen

Elle Series

I am Elle -A Psychological Thriller

Blurb:

An abused girl's desperate fight for survival and the silent killer determined to destroy her.

Born on a small farm in Alabama, Elenore Griffin spends her days in a Hell of her father's making.

The system has failed her, leaving her trapped in a world of unimaginable torture and pain.

Sold to the highest bidder, Elenore finds her nightmares have only just begun. And those responsible for her abuse begin disappearing around her without a trace, while the local authorities seem to be at the center of it all.

Step inside the world of a young girl who suffered the most heinous acts imaginable. And survived.

This is her life. This is her story...

Elle Returns– Book 2

Elle Unleashed – Book 3

The Boy in the Window

A Suspense Thriller

Blurb:

What happened to Terry Dayton?

The small community of Sparkleberry Florida is strangely tight-lipped about the disappearance of a little boy in their neighborhood. Are they covering up a thirteen-year-old murder? Jessica Nobles finds out the hard way when she moves in next door and begins unraveling the truth about 221 Meadowbrook Circle...

Jessica and Owen Nobles are heartbroken over the loss of their son, Jacob. Jessica has taken his death especially hard, spending the past three years sedated and under the care of a psychiatrist. Desperate to save his wife, Owen moves the couple to Florida, hoping a change in scenery will remind her how to live again.

When Jessica begins to see a small boy in the upstairs window of the abandoned home next door, she goes to investigate, only to find the house empty. Afraid that she may be seeing things, Jess does an internet search on the home's address. What she finds is an image of the boy from the window—a boy that's been missing more than thirteen years.

Reluctant to tell her husband, Jessica sets out to find what information she can on the child's disappearance. Yet, someone is going to great lengths to stop her.

To make matters worse, bodies begin dropping around her like flies. And she's the prime suspect in the killings. If Jessica doesn't back off now, she risks losing more than just her mind…she could very well lose her life.

The Girl Named Mud

A Gripping Suspense Novel

Blurb:

A heartbreaking story of a young girl's fight for survival in a world full of betrayal, hate, and murder...

All her life, twelve-year-old Mud has been told the Devil would be coming for her. With only her schizophrenic mother to protect her, Mud must learn to survive in the swamps of Louisiana by any means necessary.

Even if she must take a life to do it.

But then her mother is murdered in front of her...

Suddenly alone in the world, Mud takes to the streets, stealing what's required to stay alive. She knows that evil is coming, and she trusts no one. Until a chance meeting with Grace Holloway changes everything. Grace seems kind and generous, taking Mud in when no one else would. But Grace's life is also filled with secrets—dark secrets that could very well destroy them both...

The Girl Who Lived to Tell

A Chilling Thriller

Blurb:

How far would you go to stay alive?

Sandy Patterson has it all: a handsome husband who adores her and a new job teaching math at the local high school. But a dark cloud hangs over the halls. A serial killer stalks the shadows, snatching innocent teenage girls and leaving behind a string of broken and battered corpses. Not even the FBI can find this elusive murderer.

Until one fateful night, Sandy finds herself in the clutches of the same psychotic maniac who wants nothing more than to torture and demean her. Forced into a mind-bending game of life and death, Sandy races to unlock the mystery surrounding her twisted captor. But time is running out for her — and her unborn baby. To survive, she'll have to learn to think like a killer. Or become one herself…

Quick Chronicles

A Gripping Thriller Series

The Silencer – Book 1

Blurb:

Six bodies. Two serial killers. And a profiler with nothing left to lose.

Some demons refuse to stay buried. Especially when it's personal. Former FBI profiler, Oliver Quick, has spent the past six years obsessed with catching a serial killer known as the Silencer. But the trail's gone cold.

Until the FBI asks for his help on a case involving a mutilated woman found beneath the pier of a local tourist attraction.

The chase is on, with Oliver hunting not one but two serial killers. The Silencer is back, and he's toying with Quick.

Oliver finds himself trapped in a deadly game of cat-and-mouse with one of the most notorious serial killers to ever live. Will he finally catch the Silencer and put his demons to rest, or is the Hunter about to become the Hunted…

The Prophet – Book 2 - Releasing early 2020

Silence of the Whippoorwill

A Psychological Thriller

Blurb:

Vengeance is mine...

Legend has it, when the whippoorwill sings, death is soon to follow...

But Investigator Breezy Anderson doesn't believe in myths. Until a hiking trip to the mountains of Arkansas with some friends, takes a dangerous turn.

Breezy soon discovers, they're not alone. A group of crazed psychopaths are hunting them, picking them off one by one. With no hope of escape, Breezy is forced into a cat-and-mouse game of death and survival.

But her attackers made one mistake. They left her alive…

The Hitcher

A Heart-Pounding Thriller